Praise for Richard T. Ryan's Holmes' adventures

Winner of the Underground Book... Novel of the Year" Award.

Winner Silver Medal in the Readers' Favorite book-award contest.

"[*The Vatican Cameos* is] an extravagantly imagined and beautifully written Holmes story." – Lee Child, NY Times Bestselling author and the creator of Jack Reacher

"Once you've read *The Vatican Cameos*, you'll find yourself eagerly awaiting the next in Ryan's series." – Fran Wood, What Fran's Reading for nj.com

"Richard T. Ryan's *The Vatican Cameos* is an excellent pastiche-length novel, very much in the spirit of the original Holmes' stories by Sir Arthur Conan Doyle." – Dan Andriacco, author of a host of Holmes' tales as well as the blog, bakerstreetbest.com

"Loved it! A must read for all fans of Sherlock Holmes!" – Caroline Vincent, Bits about Books

"Richard Ryan channels Dan Brown as well as Conan Doyle in this successful novel." – Tom Turley, Sherlockian author

"If you enjoy deeply researched historical fiction, combined with not one but two mystery/thriller stories, then you will really enjoy this excellent Sherlock Holmes pastiche." – Craig Copland, author of New Sherlock Holmes Mysteries

"The Stone of Destiny"

"Sometimes a book comes along that absolutely restores your faith in reading. Such is the 'found manuscript' of Dr. Watson, *The Stone of Destiny*. Exhilarating, superb narrative and a cast of characters that are as dark as they are vivid. ... A thriller of the very first rank." – Ken Bruen, author of *The Guards, The Magdalen Martyrs* and many other novels, as well as the creator of the Jack Taylor

"Somewhere Sir Arthur Conan Doyle is smiling. Ryan's *The Stone of Destiny* is a fine addition to the Canon." – Reed Farrel Coleman, NY Times Bestselling author of *What You Break*

"A wonderful read for both the casual Sherlock Holmes fan and the most die-hard devotees of the beloved character." – Terrence McCauley, author of *A Conspiracy of Ravens* and *A Murder of Crows*

"Full of interesting facts, the story satisfies and may even have you believing that Holmes and Watson actually existed." – Crime Thriller Hound

"Ryan's Holmes is the real deal in [*The Stone of Destiny*]. One hopes the author is hard at work on the next adventure in this wonderfully imagined and executed series." – Fran Wood, What Fran's Reading for nj.com

"Mystery lovers will enjoy reading *The Stone of Destiny: A Sherlock Holmes Adventure* by Richard T. Ryan." – Michelle Stanley

"All in all, *The Stone of Destiny* is a captivating and intriguing detective novel and another great Sherlock Holmes adventure!" – Caroline Vincent, Bits About Books

"The Druid of Death"

"The Druid of Death is clever and fun, a winning combination. The setting —Victorian England — and the Druidic lore is absolutely captivating. This is my favorite kind of mystery." – Criminal Element

" ... the Druidic detail and the depiction of 19th-century London are fascinating and delightful." – Kirkus Reviews

"Richard Ryan has found his niche in creating new adventures for our famous detective and his sidekick." – Caroline Vincent, Bits About Books

"The Druid of Death by Richard T. Ryan is a compelling story that transported me back in time and made the iconic duo of Holmes and Watson jump off the page." – Books of All Kinds

"Where many of the tangent series have been challenged to keep these characters [Holmes and Watson] fresh, this author has accomplished not only that but made them enjoyable too." – Jennie Reads

"Ryan creates a thoroughly enjoyable pastiche, giving readers just what you'd expect from such a mystery. The suspense is tangible, and the detection methodologies quirky. He's right on the money with his characterizations of all the usual players, especially Holmes and Watson." – Barbara Searles @the bibliophage.com

"A stunning achievement!" – Ken Bruen, author of *The Guards* and creator of Jack Taylor

"Richard Ryan's latest visit to Watson's Tin Dispatch Box has discovered his best book yet and my favorite of his three novels." – David Marcum, Sherlockian author, editor and collector

"An excellent must-read for new and old friends of Mr. Holmes and Dr. Watson." – Terrence McCauley, award-winning author of *The Fairfax Incident" and Sympathy for the Devil*

"*The Druid of Death*? Sign me up! Sherlock Holmes and Dr. Watson find themselves caught in a diabolical game of cat-and-mouse as the body count starts to rise. I devoured this book in an evening; you will too." – Leah Guinn, The Well-Read Sherlockian blog

"As one would expect from a Sherlock Holmes story, the great detective's intellect, keen eye for observation, and logical deductions all play a factor in the satisfying conclusion of this mystery." – Kristopher Zgorski, founder of BOLO Books

"Sherlockians craving a new challenge for their favorite sleuth need look no further than Richard T. Ryan's *The Druid of Death*, which puts Holmes on the trail of one of his most fiendish adversaries ever." – Steven Hockensmith, author of the Edgar Award finalist *Holmes on the Range*

The Merchant of Menace

"This rousing, intriguing, devilishly fun caper, well executed and well-paced, had me hooked from the first page. The dutiful Watson, Holmes' deductive skills, and a worthy nemesis to rival the evil Moriarty himself, make this cat-and-mouse adventure a page-turning, edge-of-your-seat coaster ride well worth taking." – Tracy Clark, author of *Broken Places* and *Borrowed Time* and the creator of Cass Raines

"[In *The Merchant of Menace*], Ryan takes reality and weaves it together with Sherlockian mythology and a fun mystery. – Barbara Searles @the bibliophage.com

"[*The Merchant of Menace* is] an absolute humdinger of a novel …It is beautifully written, erudite and hugely entertaining." – Ken Bruen, the author of *The Ghosts of Galway* and the creator of Jack Taylor

"*The Merchant of Menace*, Rich Ryan's fourth Holmes novel is his most Sherlockian yet. Moving from what initially seems to be an insignificant incident to a series of crimes with international implications, Ryan present Holmes the way I like to encounter him: A true hero who is always three steps ahead of the criminal." – David Marcum, Sherlockian author, editor and collector

The Merchant of Menace:
A Sherlock Holmes Adventure

By Richard T. Ryan

Hardcover ISBN 978-1-78705-438-7
Paperback ISBN 978-1-78705-439-4
AUK ePub 978-1-78705-440-0
AUK PDF 978-1-78705-441-7

Published in the UK by MX Publishing
335 Princess Park Manor, Royal Drive, London, N11 3GX
www.mxpublishing.co.uk

Cover design by Brian Belanger.

As always this book is dedicated to my wife, Grace.
No man could ever ask for a better life partner.

It is also dedicated to my daughter, Dr. Kaitlin Ryan-Smith;
my son, Michael; my son-in-law, Daniel; and my new
granddaughter, Riley Grace.
You all know how special you are to me.

Finally, the book is a tribute to my brother-in-law,
Mark Veldhuis, and my good friend, Charlie Esposito.
Two outstanding men taken from us far too soon.

"… at the end, truth will out."
The Merchant of Venice, Act II, Scene 2

Introduction

With a great deal of time on my hands, having retired after a nearly 40-year career as a journalist, I have been indulging my passion for the printed word, both poring over manuscripts and attempting to write my own. Like Sherlock Holmes, I consider myself a "voracious reader," although my memory is not nearly as sharp as his.

One day as I was rummaging through the various cases in the tin dispatch box of Dr. Watson which I had acquired at an estate auction in Scotland, I noticed the bottom of the box seemed ever so slightly raised in one corner. Upon a closer examination, I realized that what I had believed to be the bottom of the case was actually nothing more than a thin sheet of metal which had been cut to the exact dimensions of the box. Taking a small flathead screwdriver, I was able to pry up that false bottom, and underneath I discovered this latest case, which had been hidden there.

I must admit I found the notion of Dr. Watson secreting a manuscript away in the bottom of a box – which he owned, and which many believed to be locked away safely in the vaults of Cox and Company – too fascinating to resist, so I sat down and began to read it immediately.

As readers of my past efforts are aware, the cases in this box had all been withheld from the public for various reasons, and "The Merchant of Menace" is no exception. While Holmes' vanity forestalled the publication of "The Druid of Death," and the potential political fallout in Italy and England, respectively, precluded the publication of "The Vatican Cameos" and to a lesser degree, "The Stone of Destiny," I believe the astute reader can ascertain several reasons for withholding this particular manuscript from the public.

The fact that it was so carefully concealed speaks to the embarrassment which might have fallen at the feet of any number of families and highly placed officials should it have ever been released near the time of the events.

After I had read Doctor Watson's notes a second time, I must admit that I was also somewhat hesitant about releasing this particular tale.

I am convinced, however, that this adventure deserves to be seen despite the good doctor's misgivings – as well as my own. That bit of information having been dispensed with, I caution readers this is one of the strangest cases that ever found its way to 221B Baker Street.

If, like the Great Detective, you have a taste for the *outre*, then I think you will find this tale to your liking. If nothing else, it certainly offers certain insights into the sensibilities of the late-Victorian and Edwardian eras which Holmes called home.

Richard T. Ryan

Chapter 1: London, 1901

This case, which eventually proved to be one of the most daunting tests of the true mettle of my friend, Sherlock Holmes, had its rather inauspicious beginnings in what at the time appeared to be a fairly mundane encounter.

One Monday morning in late April while I was reading the paper over breakfast, an item captured my attention. According to the article in The Guardian, a rare, jewel-encrusted dagger had been stolen from the library of Lord William Thornton. Thinking my friend might find this of some interest, I asked, "Holmes, have you read about the theft of this dagger from Lord Thornton?"

"Indeed, I have," he replied. "If it is the piece of which I am thinking, it is actually a *jambiya*. I shouldn't be surprised to learn some footman pilfered it, no doubt in order to settle his gambling debts. There is nothing there for us, I believe."

I was not surprised at my friend's lack of enthusiasm, as common crimes did little to stimulate his interest, and truth be told, he found them more tiresome than challenging. Nevertheless, I felt compelled to inquire, "A *jambiya*?"

"Surely you came across them in India?" he replied.

"Not that I can recall."

Sensing yet another opportunity to impress me with the breadth of his knowledge, and having warmed to the subject a bit, he continued, "*Jambiyas* are wide, double-edged knives that can trace their origins to Yemen. In that country, they are a symbol of social class, and I have heard it said a true Yemeni would rather die than be seen in public without his *jambiya*."

"Rather like those American cowboys and their pistols?" I ventured.

Holmes cast me a withering glance and continued as though I had not even spoken, "As is the case here, they are often embellished with gold and precious stones. Although I will admit that while I have no idea how Lord Thornton acquired his *jambiya*, I must say that people who keep such *objets d'art* around the house are simply asking for trouble. Decorations are one thing, but a trophy such as that, acquired only because you are wealthy and powerful, well, that just strikes me as little more than ostentation."

"You cannot mean that," I said, gazing around our cluttered rooms. "Look at your own collection of odds and ends littering our lodgings."

"Yes, but none of my possessions, strange and varied as they may be, was looted from a foreign country." Sweeping his arm about the room, he said, "There is nothing here that has not been earned and paid for by the sweat of my brow."

"Does that include your Stradivarius?"

Once again ignoring my jibe, Holmes continued, "At any rate, I am expecting a visit from Lestrade, regarding that self-same knife."

"And what will you tell him?"

"Look to the servants," replied my friend. "They are always among us, yet they are seldom noticed."

Thinking those would be the ideal traits of any good person in service, I returned to my paper as Holmes resumed working on a monograph he was preparing regarding tattoos and their popularity among the criminal element. Perhaps an hour later, just as I was getting ready to leave for my club, I heard the bell ring.

"I shouldn't be surprised if that were Lestrade now," said Holmes.

I decided to wait, and a moment later, there was a knock on the door. "Come in, Mrs. Hudson," my friend yelled across the room.

Our landlady entered and said, "There is a gentleman here to see you, Mr. Holmes."

I could see by the look on his face that Holmes was both genuinely surprised and pleased. "Please show him up, Mrs. Hudson." Looking at me he said, "A new client and a visit from Lestrade – this certainly has all the makings of a red-letter day."

A moment later, a tall, spare gentleman with close-cropped gray hair stepped into our rooms. After examining us both, he turned to where Holmes was standing and said in a deep, sonorous voice, "Mr. Holmes, I am William Thornton. Perhaps you have heard of me," he continued as he handed my friend his card.

Holmes replied, "To answer your question, I have heard of your missing knife and thus by extension, yourself, Lord

3

Thornton. Correct me if I am wrong, but it is a *jambiya* that has been stolen, is it not?"

Before speaking, Thornton glanced at me, and Holmes continued, "This is my friend and colleague, Dr. John Watson. You may speak freely in front of him, and I assure you he is the very soul of discretion."

Having made up his mind, Thornton continued. "It is a *jambiya* indeed, and I must say I had rather hoped to keep the theft a secret, but apparently, such things are impossible once the law has become involved."

"And with whom have you spoken from Scotland Yard? Inspector Lestrade?"

Pausing for a second, Thornton looked at Holmes and remarked, "I was told that you were rather perceptive. But yes, the fact is I have been dealing with your Inspector Lestrade, who has arrested my valet and charged him with the theft."

Glancing at me with an I-told-you-so look on his face, Holmes replied, "He is hardly my Inspector, Your Lordship. But if an arrest has been effected, then why are you here?"

"Gilbert, my valet, has been with me for more than 20 years. He would no more have taken the *jambiya* than you, Mr. Holmes."

"Do tell. Then why did Lestrade arrest him? Surely, he had evidence of some sort in order to justify the charge."

Thornton replied, "The police found a large sum of money in Gilbert's room, and after some inquiries, they learned he also owed more than five hundred pounds to a bookmaker."

After another glance in my direction, Holmes said, "I grant you that the evidence is circumstantial, but on the surface it does seem rather convincing, does it not? What does your man say for himself?"

"He admits to being in debt," said Thornton.

"And how does he explain the money?" asked Holmes.

"He refuses to say where he obtained it."

"Curious," said Holmes. "A simple explanation might free him, yet he allows himself to be incarcerated instead.

"Did anyone else have access to the *jambiya*?"

"A number of people did," replied Thornton. "The night before it was discovered missing, we hosted a small gathering at the house to celebrate my wife's birthday."

"When you say 'small,' exactly how many people are we talking about?"

"There were four other couples, in addition to my wife and myself, but they are all above suspicion. Of that, I can assure you."

"No one is above suspicion, Lord Thornton. People will do the most unexpected things for reasons that defy any type of logical explanation. May I ask where the knife came from and in what room it was kept?"

"My father was an officer in the army, serving in India as well as China during the first Opium War, and he brought the *jambiya* back from China. He would never elaborate on how the weapon had come into his possession, and since he's been dead these seven years, I suppose we will never know exactly how he came by it. However, he was inordinately fond of it, to the point where he had a special wooden holder made for the knife, and he always kept it on his desk in the library. Since his passing, I have done the same."

"Interesting," said Holmes. "One is always curious about the provenance of such items, and whether they actually belong to the person who now possesses them."

"What are you suggesting?" asked Thornton angrily.

"I am merely pointing out that we know precious little about the object in question. While it has been in your family for these many years, there may be others who believe it rightfully belongs to them."

"Possession is nine-tenths of the law," replied Thornton in a brusque tone which I could see had rubbed my friend the wrong way.

"If you are going to quote legal axioms, at least quote them correctly," said Holmes.

"I beg your pardon?" said Thornton icily.

"The actual saying is: 'Possession is nine points of the law.' And if you wish to trace that maxim to its Scottish origins, they hold that 'possession is eleven points of the law and there be but twelve.' But I fear we are digressing.

"The people at your soiree, friends and business acquaintances?" asked Holmes.

"All relatives and close friends of long duration, and I would be willing to swear that none of them took the *jambiya*."

At that point, there was a knock on the door. "Yes, Mrs. Hudson?" asked Holmes.

Poking her head inside the door, she announced, "Inspector Lestrade is here to see you, Mr. Holmes."

"By all means, show him up."

I could see Holmes was relishing the prospect of Lestrade in the same room with Lord Thornton. "Are you sure this is wise?" I whispered after Thornton had turned to stare out the window.

"We are all civilized," replied Holmes placidly. When Lestrade entered, Holmes greeted him warmly, saying, "Good afternoon, Inspector. What brings you here today?"

Even before he had fully entered the room, Lestrade caught sight of Thornton. "I have questions about a case," replied the inspector.

Looking at Thornton, Lestrade decided to seize the initiative and said, "Lord Thornton, may I remind you that I am the investigating officer on your case. Any concerns you may have should be addressed to me. There's no need to involve Mr. Holmes in this affair."

"I told you Gilbert is innocent, but you arrested him anyway," replied Thornton. "I will not stand by idly while there is a grave miscarriage of justice."

"I did not arrest Mr. Gilbert," replied Lestrade evenly. "I merely detained him at the Yard so I could question him further. He has answered all my questions satisfactorily. His story has been verified, and he has been released."

"Well, Inspector," demanded Thornton, "have you recovered the *jambiya*?"

"Not yet," replied Lestrade, "but I have my best men working on it."

"By the way, Inspector, may I inquire as to what occasioned your visit to Mr. Holmes?" asked Thornton.

"I'm afraid that is a matter of police business. Another case entirely," replied Lestrade.

"Inspector, I shall give you one week to recover my property. Mr. Holmes, if the *jambiya* is not in my possession by that time, I should like to retain you to ascertain its whereabouts and effect its recovery. I believe you have my card, sir."

"Let us cross that bridge when we come to it, Your Lordship. I do indeed have your card. Here is mine. Should anything else about the knife or the theft occur to you, please inform Inspector Lestrade. If the need should arise, I will consult with him."

"Thank you, Mr. Holmes," he said, shaking my friend's hand. Looking at myself and then Lestrade, he said, "Dr. Watson, Inspector, a good day to you both."

After he had left, Holmes looked at Lestrade and said, "Another case entirely? Prevarication hardly suits you, Inspector."

"I had to tell him something Mr. Holmes. The man has been making my life miserable. If I didn't know better, I'd swear he had something to hide himself."

"So you have come about the *jambiya*?"

Looking sheepish, Lestrade said, "I do need your help Mr. Holmes. When we had the valet down at the Yard, he informed us the money in his room had been loaned to him by Thornton's wife to cover his debts. When I braced her about it, she admitted advancing Gilbert the money and begged me to keep her secret. You may make of that what you will, but I was rather impressed by the valet's nobility."

"That's all well and good, Lestrade, but what have you learned concerning the theft?"

"That's the problem, Mr. Holmes. All of Thornton's guests and their spouses would appear to be in the clear. We can find no hidden debts or anything else unsavory about them. In fact, three of the four couples are actually better off financially than he, and the remaining couple is not wanting for anything, either."

"So, we have a stolen knife that was taken at an unspecified time by a person or persons unknown and unseen," said Holmes.

"That about sums it up," said Lestrade.

Turning to me, Holmes smiled and said, "Watson, perhaps I was mistaken in my initial assessment of the crime. There may be something of interest here yet."

"So then you'll help me, Mr. Holmes?" asked Lestrade.

"Indeed. I shall also try to be as circumspect as possible. After all, you know how much those unseen, unknown thieves hate being disturbed."

I saw Lestrade redden slightly, but since he was in need of my friend's help, he remained silent.

What none of us failed to realize at the time was that although they were uttered in jest, Holmes' words would prove to be uncannily prophetic.

Chapter 2

Over the next few days, I saw very little of my friend. As I was busy with patients and Holmes was keeping his usual odd hours, it wasn't until late Thursday afternoon that I returned home and found him, sitting in his armchair, stuffing his old clay pipe with tobacco that he kept in the Persian slipper.

"Well, you appear to have been quite busy this week," I ventured.

"Indeed, I have," he replied as he lit his pipe, "but then I might say the same thing about you."

"I make my observation on the basis of the fact that we have seen little of each other over the past several days," I stated. "How could you possibly ascertain whether I have been busy every day – or just today? I admit to the veracity of your observation, but in this instance, I am inclined to think you have made a lucky guess. After all, you have not been here, so there's been little if anything for you to observe. With nothing to scrutinize and a paucity of facts, there can be no deductions, as you have admonished me yourself upon more than one occasion."

"A touch, Watson. A definite touch, nevertheless, I fear that you are somewhat wide of the mark. Besides, as you know, I never guess."

"Then do enlighten me, my friend."

"When you entered the room just now, you were carrying your medical bag in your left hand. You do that only when it is empty or quite light because of your war wound. That tells me you were so busy today you tired of carrying it in your good arm."

"In that you are correct," I replied, "but as I have no way of knowing how long you have been here, I am willing to concede that point. What about the other three days?"

"A quick look at your boots tells me they have seen neither polish nor brush in quite some time, probably since they were last shined by the buttons on Sunday. Add to that the fact that the pile of books by the side of your chair has remained undisturbed since our visit from Lestrade, and I can only conclude that if you cannot find the time to read and are neglecting your appearance, it can only be because you have been doing something far more important. And to a physician, there is nothing that supersedes tending to the sick. Therefore, I rest my case."

"Bravo, Holmes. There is a nasty virus wreaking havoc in several sections of East London. The immigrants there, hailing as they do from Ireland and all over the Continent, including Germany, Poland and parts of Russia, appear scarce acquainted with soap and water. As a result of the unsanitary conditions and poor hygiene, the disease has been running rampant. A number of physicians have banded together to try to bring the contagion under control. It has been particularly prevalent in Whitechapel, St. George's-in-the-East and Mile End."

"Here you are saving lives and ministering to those suffering while I busy myself trying to retrieve a rather obnoxious aristocrat's precious gewgaw."

"Holmes, you are delivering justice – something all men deserve."

"Yes, you are right, I suppose."

"Come, what has put you off, old friend?"

"I compiled a list of the guests at Lord Thornton's soiree. I must say, he does move in rarefied company."

"Who was present?"

"There were, as you know, four couples, in addition to Lord and Lady Thornton. They included the Earl and Countess of Camber; The Duke and Duchess of Northrup; Richard Carlyle, the financier, and his wife; and finally, there was Lady Thornton's sister, Lucille, and her husband, Edgar Sweeney, a senior partner at Lloyd's of London."

"It doesn't sound as though any of them need worry about where their next meal is coming from," I observed.

"Quite right, Watson. And yet, the fact remains that one of those eight people pilfered Lord Thornton's *jambiya*."

"How can you be so certain?"

"After verifying with Lord Thornton that the knife was there on the day of the party, I visited the estate and examined the study where it had been displayed. There were no signs of forced entry at any of the windows. At night, they allow two rather fierce-looking mastiffs to roam the grounds as a deterrent to would-be burglars."

"How can you be certain it wasn't one of the other servants?"

"Lord Thornton keeps a staff of four, all of whom have been with him for two decades or more. While longevity of service is an admirable trait, it certainly doesn't preclude one of his staff from possessing larcenous tendencies. However, the cook was in the kitchen the entire evening preparing the meal, and the others were busy serving the guests and attending to their various needs. While they have had ample opportunity in the past to purloin the dagger, there appears to have been none on the night in question.

"Moreover, I have interviewed each of them, and I am inclined to believe they are innocent. As a result, we are left with the guests."

"But according to Lestrade, three of the four couples are more wealthy than His Lordship."

"And so they are," replied Holmes.

"Then this makes no sense. Why would anyone as well off as these people steal a treasured possession from a friend?"

"As usual, Watson, you proceed directly to the heart of the matter. Why indeed? At first thought, I can offer at least three different possible reasons."

"Really?" I exclaimed. At this point, I might have thought Holmes was indulging in a bit of braggadocio, but I had known him long enough to tell when he was deadly serious about a matter, and this was one of those instances.

"With the right motivation, anyone can be forced to betray even their closest friend. Topping the list of means that might be employed is blackmail," said Holmes in a voice of pure equanimity. "Who knows what pressure might have been exerted upon one of those individuals?"

"Yes, but they risk everything, their good name, their social standing. They would be pariahs – social lepers, as it were – and I am certain His Lordship would prosecute, so there is also the possibility of a prison sentence to consider."

After a pause, I continued, "So then the pressure brought to bear upon one of them to force that individual to commit the crime must have been extreme, yes?"

"I would say so," replied Holmes, before he added, "and that is what leads me to believe our thief is a woman."

"A woman?" I exclaimed.

"Yes, my friend. I am afraid in this instance, a member of the fairer sex, which you have so often placed on a pedestal, must be seen as having feet of clay."

"But Holmes, why a woman?"

"Let us begin by considering opportunity and then the difficulties posed by the theft."

"What exactly are you driving at?"

"Throughout the evening, all of the guests had various chances to take the *jambiya*. However, whoever stole the dagger knew that if the theft were detected that night, he or she might be searched. Now a man really has nowhere to conceal such an item, but a woman ..."

"Always carries a purse of some sort!" I exclaimed.

"Exactly. Whoever stole the dagger had to conceal it. And the hiding place had to be such that if the theft were inadvertently discovered, she would have at least a chance of leaving the premises with her ill-gotten gains. Admittedly, a man might have concealed the dagger on his person initially and perhaps hidden it with the intention of returning later to retrieve it, but that feels wrong.

"Also, none of the people there that night has returned to His Lordship's house since the theft, and I made a thorough examination of the study, sitting room and dining room as well as the water closet. No knife had been concealed in any of those places, of that I can assure you."

"So what will you do?"

"I need to question the women. In my entire career, I can think of but one woman who might have brazened it out and convinced me of her innocence even if she were guilty."

"But she was certainly not at the party," I remarked.

"True enough, but there are certain bonds that link the members of the opposite sex, and, as you know, the motives of women have always remained inscrutable to me."

While I might not have agreed with Holmes' rather disparaging remarks about women, I could find no fault in his logic nor in the means that might have been employed to spirit the ornate dagger out of the house.

"Tomorrow, I will begin making discreet inquiries about each of the women," he said.

"And just how do you propose to do that?"

"I shall start with their maids. Servants are often attuned to the sensibilities of their mistresses. We shall soon discover if anyone has been behaving oddly or acting out of sorts lately."

"Do you think the servants will confide in you?"

"Ah, but they won't be confiding in me," replied Holmes.

"You are going in disguise then?"

"I think that is best," replied my friend. "Too many people are aware of my association with the police, and I would think that some might find it rather off-putting, and as a result, an impediment to free discourse. Besides," added Holmes, adopting a perfect Scottish-English accent, "Ah hae nae intentions ay gettin' caught."

Although we laughed at the sentiment and the notion of anyone seeing through one of Holmes' disguises, we little realized the twisted path this simple theft would lead us down and the unseen perils that would present themselves along the way.

Chapter 3

My work kept me extremely busy the next day, and when I returned to Baker Street in the evening, Mrs. Hudson informed me that Holmes, dressed as she put it "in one of his silly costumes, looking for all the world like a disreputable street peddler," had returned to our rooms, eaten and then departed again "in the same sordid state in which he had arrived."

"I realize it is his job, Doctor, but perhaps you could prevail upon him to use the tradesman's entrance when he's dressed in such a manner."

"I shall do my best, but...," and I let the words trail off.

"I understand, Doctor," she said with more than a hint of resignation in her voice. "It's just that I do so like to keep up appearances."

I vowed that I would voice her concerns to Holmes the next time an opportunity presented itself. However, if Holmes returned to our lodgings that evening, he did so long after I had retired

The next day I missed him at breakfast once again. London seemed a dark and dreary place as the city was buffeted by high winds and pelted by an unrelenting rain. As I trudged home through the twilight under a leaden sky, my thoughts were focused on a warm fire, a hot meal and perhaps the companionship of Holmes.

When I entered our rooms, I could see immediately that Holmes' dour demeanor mirrored the elements.

After a moment, he roused himself and his mood changed perceptibly. Leaping from his chair, he exclaimed, "Ah, Watson, so good to see you. I trust your day has been somewhat more profitable than mine."

"So, you have made no progress in the case of the missing dagger?"

"Quite the contrary, old friend. I have learned who took it, and I know why it was stolen, but the information does me little good at present."

I replied, "I must admit to being a bit befuddled here. You say you have learned the identity of the person who stole the knife and you claim to know the motive, but you opine that knowledge does you no good?"

"Please allow me to explain," my friend said. "After having disguised myself as a street peddler, but one with a bit more wit than most, I visited the homes of all the women who had attended the party for Lord Thornton's wife.

"Having made the acquaintance of a maid or serving girl at each, I eventually turned our conversation to the subject of employers. They were only too eager to talk about the burdens of their positions. Who wanted her tea steeped exactly three minutes and not a second more nor less? Who wanted her bath water warm but not too hot?

"At any rate, each maid had her various complaints, except for Janet Hunter, who is employed by Lady Thornton's sister, Lucille. She described Mrs. Sweeney as the sweetest woman in the world, adding that she is as generous as she is kind.

But then she admitted the woman had been acting rather oddly in recent weeks and had only just returned to her usual amiable self.

"As you might imagine, my instincts were immediately aroused."

"Everybody has their good and bad days," I countered. "Look at the way that you yourself vacillate, depending upon whether you have a case to engage you."

Holmes gave me one of his knowing looks and nodded, and then he continued, "However, she also informed me that Mrs. Sweeney had altered her routine recently."

"Obviously some sort of threat had been leveled against the woman," I said. "Perhaps she has been unfaithful and was forced to steal the *jambiya* or have everything revealed to her husband."

"That is certainly one possibility," conceded Holmes. "However, the maid informed me that Mrs. Sweeney would take her son, Jonathan, her only child, to Regent's Park or the London Zoo just about every day – her schedule and the weather permitting."

"However, for the past two weeks, neither she nor her son has left their home without the accompaniment of one of the male servants, and as you are aware, we have enjoyed several days of quite pleasant weather during that period, today notwithstanding."

"You don't think …"

"I do, indeed. Unless I miss my guess, the threat was made against her son, and she did what any mother would do to protect her young."

"That is despicable! Threatening a child! But why did she not tell her husband? Certainly, he could have hired men to protect both her and the boy."

"That is to be determined," replied Holmes. "Tomorrow morning, I intend to pay a call upon Mrs. Sweeney. She may be able to deceive others, but I do not think she will be able to hoodwink me. Would you care to accompany me, Watson?"

"I should like nothing better," I replied, "but my work in the East End is not yet completed. However, I shall expect a full report tomorrow night."

Holmes gave me a rather quizzical look, and then he laughed out loud. After he had composed himself, he said rather drily, "So the tables have turned, have they? And now I am to report to you?"

At that we both began chuckling, and Holmes finally said, "Thank you, Watson. I must confess that is the best I have felt in several days."

When I returned to Baker Street the next evening, I found Holmes sitting in his chair in his favorite mouse-colored dressing gown, smoking his old clay pipe.

"I gather things did not go well with Mrs. Sweeney."

"Actually, no, they could not have gone better. As we suspected her son was the target."

"But why did she not report it?"

"That is the fascinating part, Watson. Apparently, the plan to steal the *jambiya* has been in the making for some time. She said her part in it began innocently enough about a month ago in Regent's Park. Jonathan was sailing a small boat in the lake, and she was reading on a nearby park bench, keeping one eye on the child at all times.

"When the boy returned to her at the bench, he carried a red balloon with him. When she asked where he had found it, he replied that a nice man had given it to him. She said that despite her vigilance, she had seen no one. She also admitted that she thought no further of the matter until a few days later when she and Jonathan were once again in the park. While she was reading, a man sat down next to her on the bench. Not knowing him, she initially tried to ignore him. Finally he said to her, 'Madam, I have something you must hear.' And then he proceeded to tell her in great detail exactly what he wanted her to do."

"My word," I exclaimed. "What an absolute bounder!"

"When she refused, he warned her that his reach was long and that he was patient in the extreme, and if necessary, he would wait for years – for just the right moment."

"Right moment for what, Holmes?"

"He informed her that she would steal the knife or her son would die as a consequence. Certainly not now, he said, but he also told her that she could not watch over him forever. He told her that he would perhaps hate to see a wedding ruined and a fiancée brought to tears, but if that's what it came to, it would happen that way, and the fault would be hers entirely. She was also instructed to tell no one of their encounter.

"She rushed home from the park with her son, saying nothing to anyone. She had resolved to avoid any excursions for a while and to tell her husband, who was away on business, everything as soon as he returned. However, that night as she went to tuck her son in, she discovered a red balloon tied to the boy's bedpost.

"She made inquiries, but all of the servants agreed that no one had entered the house and none would admit to placing it there. Returning to Regent's Park alone the next day, she was again accosted by the man, who reiterated exactly what he expected her to do. He even gave her a handbag that had apparently been specially constructed for the occasion."

"Could she describe the man, Holmes?"

"What details she could provide were of little use as he was quite obviously disguised. She said he was rather portly, with long, flaxen hair and a full beard and moustache. He wore dark spectacles and was perhaps six feet tall."

"Well that certainly does little to narrow it down."

"Exactly," he said in exasperation.

"How about the bag, you mentioned?"

"That might have provided a wealth of clues. Apparently, it had been constructed with a false bottom about two inches deep. The leather trim could be raised on one side, revealing a secret compartment into which she slid the *jambiya* on one of the many times she excused herself that evening. The next day, as arranged, she returned to Regent's Park at 3 p.m., left the bag on the bench where she had met the man and returned home."

"My word, Holmes! What an extraordinary story!"

"I find it more worrisome than extraordinary."

"Have you anything to work with? I mean surely this villain must be someone from her own social class as he knew not only about the upcoming party but that she had been one of the few guests."

"Ordinarily, I would agree with you, but apparently there was an article in The Times a few weeks prior, describing the planned soiree, complete with the rather exclusive guest list."

"So it could be any criminal in London then?"

"I think not. One doesn't steal an easily identifiable object unless one has a buyer for it."

"Perhaps he pried out the jewels and had the gold melted down."

"That is certainly a possibility," replied Holmes, "but he would only get a fraction of what an interested buyer might be willing to pay for the original *jambiya* intact. No, Watson, our thief is a middleman of sorts, a broker if you will. He does not steal randomly; in fact, he does not steal at all, if he can avoid it, and that is the genius of his plan.

"He has others carry out his dirty work while he remains safely out of harm's way – and of the clutches of the law."

"You say 'others.' Has he done this sort of thing before?"

"I am certain that he has, but we were never aware of this person's existence until today.

"Now, I must do some research." With that my friend dragged out the first volume of his "good old index" and began to read through the clippings he had amassed over the years.

Knowing that to disturb him was pointless, I dined alone, watching him as I ate. After a few hours, I realized Holmes was not to be dissuaded from his self-appointed task that evening, so I left him to his research while I enjoyed the poetry of Matthew Arnold. After I had read for a while, I made an early night of it and turned in. As I lay in bed, I kept wondering what type of man would threaten a child in order to achieve his end. In turn, that led me to reflect upon some of our past cases and the various ne'er-do-wells we had encountered. Although my sleep was fitful, the morning seemed bright and full of promise with the sun streaming through my windows.

As I entered our sitting room, I saw that Holmes was sitting in his chair, perusing the morning papers. "Did your research prove profitable?"

"It is too soon to tell," Holmes replied. "Over the past 18 months, I have discovered at least three other incidents that would appear to be the work of the mastermind behind the theft of Lord Thornton's knife."

"And why were you never called in to investigate?"

"Actually, in two of the instances, I was. However, thinking that they were little more than common thefts, I decided not to involve myself. I think Watson, there is a lesson there somewhere about jumping to conclusions."

"You would not have become involved in this case either, had Lord Thornton not called upon you."

"Too true. I have been an ass," he said.

"There was a pattern there, but I missed it because I violated my own rule about theorizing in advance of the facts. Well, now I must attempt to make amends for past sins and see if I can link these cases to the present problem."

Looking at me, Holmes smiled enigmatically and said:

"And we are here as on a darkling plain

Swept with confused alarms of struggle and flight,

Where ignorant armies clash by night."

"What a coincidence!" I exclaimed. "I was just reading the poetry of Matthew Arnold last night.

"Hardly a coincidence, my friend. You left the book of poetry on the floor next to your chair. Although I much prefer Donne's handling of the notion of man's isolation, no one can deny the brilliance of 'Dover Beach.'"

I was rather stunned to hear Holmes discourse on poetry, but then I had learned over the years that my friend was, if nothing else, full of surprises.

"And now, I must set out to discover whether Lady Falkland's brooch was merely misplaced or perhaps, as I suspect, stolen. Hers was one of the cases that I dismissed as a common theft. So now, I must do my best to atone for my hubris."

He paused and then added, "If you have not made plans for today, perhaps you would care to accompany me."

I said that I would be delighted, and a short time later, we found ourselves in Knightsbridge at the home of Lady Elizabeth Falkland. While we waited in the sitting room, Holmes prowled about, examining everything.

After we had been kept waiting for some fifteen minutes, Lady Elizabeth entered the room. Now in her late 50s or early 60s, she was still a striking woman. Tall and graceful with an imperious air and eyes of stunning blue.

Looking at Holmes, she said, "I understand you wish to question me about my brooch that has gone missing."

"Indeed," said Holmes. "When exactly did you first become aware of the absence of the brooch?"

"Sometime in the middle of March of last year," she replied. "I remember wearing it to the theatre on March 5, my birthday, and then when I went to wear it on March 17, I was unable to find it. After searching the entire house, I notified Scotland Yard."

"So had you not decided to wear it that evening, the theft might have remained undiscovered for some time."

"I suppose so," she replied. "It is not my favorite piece, but it was the last gift my husband gave me before he passed away."

"I'm so sorry to hear that," I replied. "I suppose the sentimental value makes it priceless."

"Only to me," she replied. "It was insured, and I have since collected on the policy."

"Would Your Ladyship be so kind as to describe the brooch for us?" asked Holmes.

"It is what they call an acrostic brooch," she replied. "They have rather fallen out of fashion now, but it is still a handsome piece."

"An acrostic brooch?" I asked.

Looking at me as though I were a simpleton, Her Ladyship explained, "The brooch itself was made of gold, but the stones were arranged in a special order. From left to right, it contained a ruby, emerald, garnet, amethyst, a second ruby and a diamond. The first letters of the stones spelled out the word REGARD. Perhaps it seems overly sentimental to you gentlemen, but it meant the world to me when I received it."

"During that period from March 5th, when you last wore it, until the 17th, when you discovered it missing, did you host any teas or parties of any kind?"

Looking at Holmes with an almost pitying expression, she replied, "Mr. Holmes, there were several soirees and get-togethers of various types that took place here. After all, it was the very height of the season."

Rising himself up, Holmes looked at her and replied icily, "Madam, I am well-aware of 'the season.' I merely wished to ascertain whether your house was the site of such gatherings as attend it and whether possibly the thief was here at one of your celebrations by invitation. I don't suppose you would still have copies of the guest lists?"

Her Ladyship looked at Holmes with a new-found respect and simply said, "Thank you, Mr. Holmes, but I am afraid the guest lists would have done you little good."

"And why is that?"

"For every 10 people you invite, there are at least five who were never invited but show up as escorts, and some others always manage to inveigle their way past the butler."

"I understand completely," said Holmes, having regained his equanimity.

"I must say, Mr. Holmes. You are very different from the other detectives with whom I have had the misfortune to deal."

Taking her remark as a compliment, whether it was intended that way or not, Holmes replied, "Thank you, Your Grace. Now I just have but one small request, if you would be so kind."

"And what is that, pray tell?" she asked.

"If you could assemble a list of any of your friends who might have attended any of the gatherings and who happen to have young children, it might go a long way in facilitating this investigation. When you have finished, please forward it to me at 221B Baker Street."

"I shall set to it at once," she replied.

Taking that as our cue, Holmes thanked Lady Falkland; then he and I wished her a pleasant day, and we soon found ourselves in a cab headed for the residence of Lady Frances Darbent. Hers was the second case about which Holmes had been contacted but had failed to act on.

She had been the proud owner of one of the few copies of William Blake's "The First Book of Urizen," which had mysteriously disappeared from her library some eight months earlier.

Upon meeting Lady Darbent, I was struck by the woman's beauty as well as her obvious strength of character. Attired in a fashionable blue costume, she was perhaps 40, and had been blessed with long raven tresses that complimented her light green eyes. All told, she offered quite a striking contrast, both in appearance and demeanor, to Lady Falkland.

After introductions had been made, she asked, "To what do I owe the honor of having the great Sherlock Holmes and his Boswell call upon me?"

"I understand that you had a rather rare book purloined from your library," replied Holmes.

"Have you found it?" she asked excitedly.

"Not yet, madam, but I am hopeful," replied Holmes. "What can you tell me about the book itself?"

"It was a rather small book," she said. "I should guess that it was less than six inches long and perhaps four inches wide."

"So then it might be easily concealed," said Holmes.

"Oh yes," she said. "It is only 48 pages long, but so beautifully illustrated. The book was originally printed in 1794, and is one of the major pieces, and perhaps the most important, in the poet William Blake's series of prophetic works."

"May I see where the book was kept?" Holmes asked.

"Certainly," replied Lady Darbent. As she escorted us to the library, it was quite obvious that she was in her element discussing books. She said, "In the book, Blake offered his rather unorthodox version of the Creation and the fall. It was written in an attempt to satirize the traditional accounts in Genesis and *Paradise Lost*. However, what makes the book so incredibly valuable is that it was one of Blake's books which featured what he had termed 'illuminated printing.' I don't pretend to be an expert, but from what I can understand, Blake's copper plates contained both the text and the images, and he would pass each leaf through his press twice, once to print the text and a second time to print the images."

At that point, we entered what I can only describe as the most magnificent library I had ever seen in a private home. The room was two stories high, and both levels featured shelves, running from floor to ceiling, filled with books and the occasional antique. In each of the various rows, there was also a ladder on wheels, allowing access to the uppermost shelves. Off in the corner was a wrought-iron circular staircase so that one might easily access the second story. On the few spots on the walls not covered by shelves, there were small recesses containing various small sculptures and other pieces.

"This is breathtaking," I remarked.'

"Collecting was a passion of my grandfather's," she explained. "He passed his love of books onto my father, and I inherited that same fondness for the printed word from him."

In addition to the shelves of books, there were two different display cases and several ornately carved tables where holders were tasked with displaying individual volumes for the perusal and enjoyment of those passing by.

Pointing to one of the tables in the center of the room, Lady Frances said, "That was where 'The Book of Urizen' was displayed. It was one of the crown jewels of the collection, and as such, it merited that pride of place."

According to Lady Frances, only eight copies of the book were known to exist, and that one had been in her family for more than a century as some distant relative had been a close friend of the poet. One day as she was entertaining visitors in her sitting room, someone asked about the book. When she took the group into the library, she discovered a similar looking book had been switched for the original. She had no idea when the substitution might have occurred, but she admitted that she was fond of entertaining, and the library was seldom locked.

When Holmes asked to see the book that had been left, she replied that an officer from Scotland Yard had taken it away as evidence. "I would be in your debt, Mr. Holmes, if you could find and return my book. I feel as though I have let my family down by allowing it to slip from my possession."

"I shall do all within my power to see that 'The Book of Urizen' is returned to its rightful owner," replied Holmes. "Can you think of anything else that might be helpful?" he inquired.

"As you know, I was devastated by the theft, but I remember thinking at the time that it was rather odd."

"Why do you say that?" asked Holmes.

"As you can see," she said, gesturing to the rest of the library, I own thousands of books. 'Urizen' was just one of my treasures. Among other notable items, my grandfather had acquired were an illustrated first edition of *Paradise Lost* and a first edition of Dr. Johnson's Dictionary; however, the most valuable piece in the collection is a First Folio of the works of Shakespeare."

"My word," I exclaimed. "And you keep them here?"

"Not any longer," she replied. "Ever since 'Urizen' was stolen, those books and a number of others are on loan to the British Library, where they are kept under lock and key at all times."

"I commend your caution," said Holmes, "but earlier you said that something struck you as being 'odd.' Do you remember what it was?"

Looking at Holmes, she answered rather cautiously, "Yes, of course. I recall thinking that with all the illustrious authors on display here, why steal a book by Blake. There are many others that might have fetched a great deal more money from any number of collectors."

"You certainly raise an interesting point, Lady Darbent. I shall have to give that some thought. By the way, might I ask a small favor of you?"

"Certainly, Mr. Holmes."

"Would you make a list of all your friends who have visited you here that have young children? If you would be so kind as to send it to me at 221B Baker Street when you have compiled it, I should be in your debt."

Looking at me, she laughed and said, "Thanks to Dr. Watson, I am well aware of your address. You shall have the list no later than tomorrow."

That said, we bid Lardy Darbent farewell. As we strolled along the street in search of a cab, I remarked, "Aside from seeing perhaps the greatest private library in the kingdom, I thought that was a rather unproductive visit."

"Really," replied my friend, "I found it singularly enlightening in several respects."

When I pressed him, he would only say, "You know my methods, Watson. You saw what I saw; you heard what I heard. See if you can't stumble upon the singular fact provided by Lady Darbent that may yet prove invaluable in solving this case."

Chapter 4

When I awoke the next morning, I discovered that Holmes had once again already breakfasted and departed. Left to my own devices, I was determined to, if not beat Holmes at his own game, then at least effect a draw. Certain that I was alone, I filled my pipe with his tobacco and donned Holmes' mouse-colored dressing gown, whereupon I sat in my friend's chair, drew up my knees, steepled my fingers under my chin, and tried to imagine myself in his shoes.

I reviewed all the interviews from the previous day, looking for anything I might have missed. I found little in our *tete-a-tete* with Lady Falkland that might be of use. As I sat there pondering our conversation with Lady Darbent, the thought that I had missed something kept nagging at me. However, the more I tried to bring it into focus, the more it eluded me. My reveries were interrupted by a knocking on the door.

"Who is it?" I asked.

"I've just received a letter by messenger for Mr. Holmes," Mrs. Hudson replied.

"Please slide it under the door if you will; I'm a bit preoccupied at the moment, Mrs. Hudson."

"As you wish, Doctor," she replied, and suddenly a long white envelope appeared on my side of the door.

"Thank you, Mrs. Hudson." After I heard her descend, I picked up the envelope and examined it. I could tell from the handwriting it had been composed by a woman. I wondered, which of the two had been so prompt, and decided that it must have been Lady Darbent. Returning to the chair, I once again assumed the position so often favored by Holmes and continued my ruminations.

Perhaps an hour later, I again heard Mrs. Hudson ascending the stairs. After knocking, she announced, "Another letter has just arrived for Mr. Holmes."

Feeling rather foolish now, I doffed Holmes' gown, throwing it over his chair, and answered the door. She handed me another long envelope, quite similar to the first, the only difference being the tint of the paper was more ivory than white. "Thank you, Mrs. Hudson," I said. "You may rest assured that I will give them to Holmes as soon as he returns."

"Will he be joining you for lunch?" she asked.

"I really can't say. You know the irregular hours Holmes keeps."

"Well, I'll prepare for two in case he should return." Casting a sideways glance in my direction as she left, she added curtly, "I'm certain it will not go to waste."

Since I knew that I had gained a little weight recently, I decided to ignore her remark. I then set about considering the latest letter. Again, the handwriting was most definitely feminine, and I was wondering which missive had been sent by whom. Holding them next to each other and then putting them on the table side by side, I picked up Holmes' lens and began to examine them closely. I was so preoccupied with my contemplation of them that I was quite startled to hear my friend proclaim: "The one on the right is from Lady Falkland."

"Holmes, you have to stop sneaking up on me like that."

He just smiled, so I continued, "Obviously, it took no great leap of your uncanny abilities to deduce what I was doing just now, but how could you possibly know, without even seeing the handwriting, which letter came from Lady Falkland?"

"When we visited her yesterday, there were several envelopes exactly like that one sitting on the desk behind her, which she presumably intended to post later in the day. There was also a quire of similar-colored paper on the desk. I remember being struck by the ivory hue, and now one arrives here the day after our visit. Child's play, Watson, even for you."

Having hung up his coat, he looked at his chair, picked up his dressing gown and remarked, "Odd! I could have sworn I had hung this up."

"And where have you been all day?" I asked, endeavoring to change the subject. "Have you learned anything new?"

"I have indeed made some headway, though I am loath to describe it as progress. The information which I acquired today confirms one of my suspicions. Now, let us examine the contents of these letters, and see if they shed any further light upon the subject." Taking a letter opener, Holmes slit the envelopes and removed a sheet of paper from each. He read them over once, muttered something under his breath which I could not discern, and then threw himself into his chair as he continued to pore over them.

Finally, he said, "It is rather what I was fearing."

"And what is that?" I asked.

"Mrs. Sweeney appears on neither list, which I expected. What's more confounding, however, is the fact that the two lists have not a single name in common."

"I should think, given the difference in age between Lady Falkland and Lady Darbent that is rather to be expected."

"True enough," said Holmes.

"But what does it mean, Holmes?"

"It means that each theft has been committed by a different person."

"Has he blackmailed three different women, then?"

"Three different people, Watson. Though they may all have been women that would be getting ahead of myself."

"But you asked Lady Darbent and Lady Falkland only about friends they might have with small children."

"We have to start somewhere. Now that we know that women with children is not the common link – although it may still prove to be a significant factor – we have to broaden the scope of our investigation or perhaps take it in another direction entirely."

"Whatever do you mean?"

"I have described our thief as a middleman, but that's not quite right. He is a great deal more than that. He is, if you will, a merchant."

"A merchant?" I asked; my confusion was obvious I am certain.

"Yes, exactly. He takes orders and then delivers the product requested for a certain price."

"My word, Holmes."

"It's commerce, Watson, plain and simple. You go to your tailor and you order a suit. He takes your measurements, buys the material and other necessary items. He then toils over your trousers, waistcoat and jacket, creating it, with only your measurements as guidelines. When he is finished, he contacts you; whereupon, you return to his shop to try it on. If everything has worked out accordingly, and you are satisfied with the fit, you pay him and your business is concluded – unless of course, you should desire another suit.

"In much the same manner, our criminal meets with his customers, takes their orders and is paid when he delivers the object in question. The only difference is that while your business with the tailor is all perfectly legal and above board, his is anything but."

"Holmes, you can't be serious?"

"And why not? We have thefts every day where people steal items for any number of reasons. All we are looking at here is a thief for hire, albeit a very clever one. If you think I am mistaken, ask Lord Thornton, Lady Falkland or Lady Darbent. Better yet, ask all three."

"But this is obviously not your garden variety thief, Holmes. If he steals on commission, how will you catch him when you have no idea what his next assignment may be or where or when it will take place?"

"As always, Watson, you cut to the heart of the matter. Since we cannot predict his movements with even the slightest degree of certainty, we must endeavor to find some means of controlling them."

"Holmes, I can see exactly where you are heading, and I must say, I do not like it."

"Watson, at best, you have but a vague idea of my direction. If you were truly aware of 'exactly' what I am envisioning, you might think that I had gone quite insane. No, old friend, I know precisely where I should like to end up – clapping a pair of darbies around this rascal's wrists and then attending his trial and sentencing. However, I fear that it is going to be quite some time, and it will require a great many moves before we are even close to bringing this so-called 'merchant' to justice.

"And now let us enjoy the lunch that Mrs. Hudson has prepared for us. Afterwards, I have several calls to make, and I am particularly interested in learning a few details about a different brooch about which I have been hearing a great deal lately."

Despite my repeated inquiries, Holmes would divulge nothing further, and after we had finished, he said, "I know you mean well, old friend. However, I have charted myself a rather treacherous course. I rather think Homer had it right when he had Odysseus choose to sail closer to Scylla than Charybdis. If you recall, Odysseus lost but a few sailors to that monster, rather than possibly losing his entire ship in the whirlpool that was Charybdis.

"Reluctantly, for at least the next part of the journey, I fear I must sail alone. I should never forgive myself if anything were to happen to you. When the immediate danger has passed, I shall be happy to have you take up your duties as my first-mate once again."

I was not to be put off so lightly, so I said, "I am touched by your concern, my friend, but we have been down this road on so many other occasions. If it is all the same to you, I would rather be by your side, than sitting here wondering what predicament you might have got yourself into."

Holmes looked at me and smiled. Then he said, "Good old Watson."

As we went out the door and descended the stairs, I must confess that despite my brave words, I was filled with misgivings and fear for my friend, and I was glad I had been able to change his mind.

Holmes hailed a cab and gave the driver an address in Bedford Square. "Are we going to the British Museum?"

"Eventually," replied Holmes. "As you have ascertained, we will be quite near it, and I am hoping to kill two birds with one stone as it were. As a matter of fact, why don't you go on ahead to the British Museum and see if our friend, Dr. Steven Smith, is in. I shall be along presently."

"You aren't trying to get rid of me again?" I asked.

"Not at all. I am merely endeavoring to save a bit of time. When you get there, make certain that you and Dr. Smith are alone and then ask him what plans have been made to secure and display the Tara Brooch."

Although I had no idea to what Holmes was referring, I agreed, albeit somewhat reluctantly. When we arrived in Bedford Square, Holmes alighted from the cab and paid the driver, asking how much more it would cost to take me to the museum.

"It's right around the corner, Mr. 'Olmes. No charge as I was going there anyway in search of me next fare." Despite the driver's protestations, Holmes tossed another coin up to him, and then he turned and walked away before the driver could toss it back.

A minute later, I found myself ascending the steps and asking one of the guards if he knew where I might find Dr. Steven Smith. After a rather lengthy walk, I found Dr. Smith in his office in the basement. I informed his secretary that although I did not have an appointment, I was fairly certain Dr. Smith would make an exception in my case.

Holmes and I had first met Dr. Smith during the case I have titled "The Druid of Death." An expert on Anglo-Irish literature and history, he had proven invaluable during our investigation, and it was his knowledge of the prehistoric writing system of ogham that had helped Holmes wrap up that nasty bit of business.

A minute later, Smith burst through his door, grabbing my hand, he said, "Dr. Watson, it is so good to see you again!" Looking about, he enquired, "Is Mr. Holmes not with you?"

"He will be along presently," I replied. "In the meantime, I do have one or two questions that Holmes would like you to answer."

"Certainly," he replied. Ushering me into his cluttered office, he removed some papers from a chair in front of his desk so that I might sit. He had almost taken his seat when he said, "And you are certain that Mr. Holmes will be joining us?"

"I expect him shortly."

He then returned to the front of the desk and removed a second, larger pile of papers and books from another chair so Holmes would have a place to sit when he arrived.

After he had finally taken his seat, Smith looked at me and said, "I am sorry the office is in such disarray, but things have been quite hectic here the past few weeks."

"Oh, why is that?"

"We are getting ready to open an exhibit of ancient Irish artifacts next month. So we have been busy ordering special display cases and deciding how best to show the collection off in such a way that we do these creations justice. We have tried to keep things secret until the formal announcement so that is why you probably haven't heard of it."

My next words appeared to stun Smith who could only look at me in a state of amazement after I asked, "Would one of those creations be the Tara Brooch? And if it is, Mr. Holmes would like to know what plans you have made to secure and protect the brooch when you display it."

Chapter 5

Owing to the look of utter astonishment on Dr. Smith's face, I realized I had shocked the man – and quite badly.

Recovering himself a bit, he looked at me and said, "How could you know anything about the Tara Brooch? It is one of the exhibit's most closely guarded secrets, and nothing has been announced."

"Dr. Smith, let me assure I know nothing about the piece in question, I was merely instructed by Holmes to ask you that question when we were alone."

"But how did Mr. Holmes come to learn of its impending presence here and the museum's plans?"

I started to answer, "I cannot presume to speak for Mr. Holmes ..." when I was cut off by a knock at the door, which the secretary opened to announce, "Mr. Sherlock Holmes to see you, Dr. Smith."

Holmes then strode into the office and taking stock of the situation, said, "I can see that you were unprepared for my colleague's question, Dr. Smith."

"Mr. Holmes, the upcoming exhibit of Celtic artifacts has not been finalized, and negotiations are still being conducted with the Irish government to iron out some of the specifics. Since you seem to know so much already, I can only conclude that you are aware that the safety of all the pieces on loan has been a bone of contention, and the Tara Brooch has been at the center of the controversy."

"Why such concern now?" asked Holmes. "The brooch has been abroad before. It was on display at the Great Exhibition in this very city in 1851 and the Exposition Universelle in Paris in 1855."

"Apparently, there have been at least three separate attempts to steal the brooch from the Irish Academy in the last year alone, and the Irish government is demanding assurances that it will be returned without incident. After all, it has become something of a rallying point for the Irish people, what with the renewed interest in Celtic history and traditions."

At the mention of the attempted thefts, I noticed a distinct change in Holmes' demeanor. In the most nonchalant manner possible, he continued, "Yes, I understand all that, but you and I both know that the legend of the Tara Brooch which has helped spur the Celtic Revival has been largely fashioned out of whole cloth."

"Be that as it may, Mr. Holmes. Her Majesty Queen Victoria always had a special fondness for the piece, to the point that she had a copy made for herself a number of years ago, and it is only because of royal intervention that the Irish government is even considering allowing us to display it."

"Do the Irish authorities have any idea who might be responsible for the attempted thefts?"

"No, and that is one of their major concerns. They believe that all of the attempts were the work of very clever professionals, and had not the brooch been secreted away in a special vault each night, the scoundrels might well have succeeded in their efforts."

"So then, to return to my original question, what steps have you taken to safeguard the brooch and the various other items while they are on display?"

Dr. Smith then outlined all the measures the museum was planning to put in place, including purchasing reinforced doors with windows made of Siemens glass and the latest locks to be placed at the entrance to the gallery; the installation of bars on the gallery windows, which were also being replaced with Siemens glass; and the presence of armed guards in the gallery around the clock. He also said that special shatterproof display cases were being constructed for the Tara Brooch and several other objects.

After he had finished his description, even Holmes looked impressed. "I must say that you appear to have thought of everything. You are aware that the new laminated glass of which you speak will slow down a thief, but it is by no means impenetrable – especially if a burglar has the right tools and a strong sense of determination."

"I am. However, Mr. Holmes," Smith continued, "the museum has also hired a security firm from America with a sterling reputation to transport the artifacts here and then to oversee and inspect all of the changes."

Once again, I saw a distinct change in Holmes' expression as Dr. Smith informed him about the American firm.

"Do you trust me, Dr. Smith?"

"Of course I do, Mr. Holmes."

Leaning forward, Holmes said to Dr. Smith, "Your security has already been breached to an uncertain degree. The fact that you seemed taken aback that I knew the Tara Brooch was coming here is just one indication. The person who informed me of its pending arrival is not connected with the museum in any way, nor is she affiliated with any security firm, and if she knows, you can be certain there are untold others who are aware of the upcoming exhibition."

"How serious is the problem?" asked Smith.

"I believe it to be quite serious; however, if you are willing to follow my instructions, we may yet foil any attempt to steal the brooch and perhaps bring an extremely evil man to justice."

"Just tell me what it is you want me to do, Mr. Holmes."

My friend proposed to develop a plan that would ensure the safety of the Tara Brooch, but it was, he admitted, a scheme that was still in its infancy.

Having been privy to many of Holmes' various plans over the years, I fully expected the end result to be something that would either be regarded as inspired or insane, depending upon your point of view. After Holmes had finished speaking, one could easily discern the uncertainty on Dr. Smith's face. He was torn between his faith in Holmes and his obvious duty to follow the orders of his superiors. Eventually though, he stood up tall and proclaimed: "Whatever you decide, I am at your disposal, Mr. Holmes. I may not like it, but I will do it."

"If anything should go wrong," Holmes said, "I will assume full responsibility. The difficulty is, there may be significant changes involved, and we may be hard-pressed to have everything in place on time. After all, we have little more than a month until the grand opening."

"You can count on my full cooperation – no questions asked," said Smith resolutely.

After shaking hands and reminding him of the importance of absolute secrecy, Holmes and I left the museum. As we descended the steps, I said, "It seems to me that you are risking a great deal, including your reputation, on one throw of the dice."

"Hardly one throw, Watson. That plan is merely one of the precautions I hope to put in place. You must remember we are dealing with an inordinately resourceful thief who is as ruthless as he is bold and will therefore stop at nothing to achieve his goals. As a result, we must be every bit as daring and cunning as he is. If I am right, we shall have launched our first counter-attack. I only pray that Dr. Smith does not waver from the course we have charted."

As we left the museum I must confess that I had serious misgivings about my friend's plan, but I could also see the rationale behind it. I only hoped that others would be as discerning – and forgiving – should anything go awry. Holmes then hailed a cab, and we set out for Baker Street.

During the ride, I asked Holmes where he had been while I was meeting with Dr. Smith.

He answered rather cryptically, "I visited an old friend of mine who dabbles in rarities and antiques."

"Is he honest? Can you trust him?"

"Honest is such a relative term, Watson. And your 'he' is, in fact, a she. Madam Isabella Cocilovo-Kozzi knew all about the upcoming exhibit; in fact, she was the one who first informed me about it several days ago."

"Then let me rephrase my question so there is absolutely no ambiguity. The woman you met, this Isabella, is she a law-abiding citizen in every aspect of her business?"

"Bravo, Watson! Well put! Consider though, who abides by the letter of the law in every aspect? My friend is very Continental, and because of that she is more attuned to the spirit of the law than the letter."

"Holmes, over the years you have had some rather questionable acquaintances. Your 'friend' Porlock comes to mind immediately. Does this Isabella fall into that category?"

Holmes gave me a rather pained look and replied. "I suppose there are a few instances when she too has crossed the line, but overall, she has rendered me such invaluable assistance on any number of occasions that I am rather inclined to overlook her periodic transgressions – so long as they remain relatively minor.

"I went to see this woman because I believed she might provide me with a list of those collectors who would be willing to go to great lengths to obtain a copy of 'The First Book of Urizen.' Although she trades in all manner of antiques, her first love is the printed page."

"And did she cooperate?"

Pulling a paper from his inside pocket, Holmes said, "She gave me a list of 10 names. These are people who, in her opinion, not only have the means to purchase such a book, were it to become available, but who also possess the inclination and financial wherewithal to take the initiative and hire someone to obtain it for them, should it remain off the market."

"So, now you have a lead of sorts?"

"I fear it may point us to a dead end; nevertheless, it is a starting point. Quite frankly, I am more concerned about whether our buyer can be persuaded to disclose the identity of his supplier – should he even know it."

After considering the possibilities, I said, "Yes, I imagine he would be rather loath to do so. After all, anyone now admitting that he had the book in his possession would find himself in a rather precarious legal position. And if he is a collector, he is not about to divulge the name of the seller because that would end their relationship. Moreover, should the betrayal ever come to light, it would certainly preclude any future dealings, and it might even spur this merchant to seek retribution."

"And so you see the problem before us, Watson, Rather a vexing one, wouldn't you say?"

"I would have to agree with you there, Holmes."

"Still, vexing is not the same as insurmountable," he said. I glanced at him, and my face must have revealed the surprise I was feeling at his last remark.

"Think of it as just another pretty little problem," he said. Holmes then lapsed into silence as he often did when he was working out various scenarios. So engrossed in his own thoughts was he that he never even noticed we had arrived at our destination.

"Come on, old boy," I said. "It is nearly dinner time. Let us see what Mrs. Hudson has prepared."

As we ascended the stairs and entered our room, Holmes sniffed the air and said to me, "I believe Mrs. Hudson has outdone herself this evening." Despite his praise, he barely touched the steak and kidney pie, and so we passed our dinner in near silence. After the dishes had been cleared, he threw himself into his favorite chair, filled the old clay pipe with shag and drawing his knees up to his chin sat there smoking like some sort of foreign idol. After the room had become filled with smoke, I knew that Holmes was continuing to play out various possibilities in his head. Having had my few cursory attempts at conversation rebuffed, I decided to visit my club and perhaps play some billiards with Thurston.

When I returned a few hours later, Holmes was still sitting in his chair. But sitting opposite him was a younger man who was every bit as tall as Holmes though a bit heavier. He had brown hair and eyes and a neatly trimmed beard and mustache.

"Watson, I should like to introduce you to Mr. Scott Dell'Osso."

"Pleased to meet you," I said. "May I ask what occasions your visit to Baker Street?"

Looking at Holmes, who nodded, Dell'Osso turned to me and said, "I believe I can lead you to the man who is now in possession of 'The First Book of Urizen.'"

Chapter 6

Turning back to my friend, Dell'Osso asked, "Shall I continue, Mr. Holmes?"

Holmes nodded, and after turning his attention to me, Dell'Osso began, "I own a small shop near the British Museum. It came to my attention earlier today that Mr. Holmes had visited a mutual friend who owns a shop quite near mine, inquiring about a certain book by William Blake. A few months ago, a man entered my premises and asked if I might be able to authenticate what he believed to be a first edition by Blake.

"I knew nothing of the theft at the time, so I agreed. After we had negotiated a fee, he returned to my shop the following day with the book in question."

"And was it 'The Book of Urizen'?" I asked.

"Indeed," said Dell'Osso. "The workmanship was flawless, and the plates were in perfect condition. I inquired if he had any interest in selling it. He merely laughed and said to me, 'I have gone to great pains and considerable expense to acquire this for my collection. Besides, I have already promised it to another buyer should I ever decide to sell.'

"I told him that if he should change his mind or his plans should fall through, I would be willing to match whatever anyone else might offer as well as an additional 10 percent. He promised to keep me informed. He then left my shop with the book and a letter signed by me attesting to its authenticity."

"And has he returned to your shop since then?" asked Holmes.

"No, but if he does, I shall let you know immediately, Mr. Holmes."

"Is there nothing else you can tell us about this man?" asked Holmes.

"I have given you his description," replied Dell'Osso. "I can also say that he was quite circumspect."

"Why do you say that?"

"He had provided me with his name and address, both of which I now know to be false."

"You can't be serious," I replied.

"Sadly, I am, Doctor. You see a few weeks later, I had the good fortune to acquire a first edition of Swift's 'A Modest Proposal.' Using it as a pretense to call upon Mr. Flood, for so he called himself, I journeyed to Torquay and was stunned to discover that the address he had provided was inhabited by a family named O'Doul, and that the house has been in their family for more than two centuries."

"So, you really have nothing to offer other than the fact that you carried out an appraisal for a man who appears to have hoodwinked you in almost every respect?" said Holmes.

"Actually, no. You see you are not the only one who observes trifles, Mr. Holmes," replied Dell'Osso evenly. "In my profession, the tiniest of ink marks, a variant spelling, transposed letter or misplaced punctuation mark may well be the only clues

55

as to whether a book or manuscript is truly an original or nothing more than a clever forgery."

"What are you trying to say?" I asked.

"During my meetings with the gentleman in question, I noticed two rather distinctive features about his appearance. Now, he wore a coat with the collar turned up and his hat was pulled low in an effort to conceal his face. He also wore tinted glasses that prevented me from ascertaining the actual color of his eyes. He was quite thin, fairly short of stature and perhaps 60 years old and clean-shaven. And while it is true that I cannot tell you his real name, I can tell you those features I observed which, taken together with everything else you know about him, should make your search somewhat easier, I think."

I was about to inform Dell'Osso that we knew virtually nothing else about the man, but Holmes shot me a reproving glance, so I remained silent.

"And what do you stand to gain from helping us?" asked my friend.

"I believe a rather sizable reward has been offered for the book's return, plus there will be my usual fee for authenticating the volume in question when it is returned, should Lady Darbent desire such authentication. Finally, I should like an introduction to Lady Darbent. Who knows, perhaps she will feel a sense of indebtedness and retain me to oversee all her future acquisitions."

"Anything else?" asked Holmes.

"No, Mr. Holmes. Although I am a businessman, I too, like you, am on the side of the angels."

"Done," said Holmes.

Dell'Osso then proceeded to describe once again in great detail all the other physical characteristics, including what he called the man's rather "plummy" accent, which he had observed about his one-time customer as well as two additional telling facts.

"My visitor sported a rather distinctive watch fob," said Dell'Osso, which he then described in great detail. "To complement that trinket, he also wore a rather unusual signet ring on the middle finger of his right hand adorned with the same emblem as the fob."

Holmes then had him recount both meetings a second time. As he described the encounters again, Holmes peppered him with questions. When Dell'Osso had finished some ten minutes later, I could see from his movements and gestures that Holmes was quite pleased, though a stranger might not have picked up on such subtle hints.

After Dell'Osso had departed, Holmes looked at me and asked, "What do you make of our enterprising antiquarian?"

"I don't like him," I said. "He's trying to turn a profit from a crime."

"A crime he didn't commit," said Holmes, who paused and then continued, "And how does that make him different from the journalists who report on such things? In fact, how different is he from you? After all, your stories about our adventures turn a tidy profit from the criminal activities of others. Unless, of course, I am mistaken."

"Blast it, Holmes! Must you always look at everything so analytically?

"I do apologize, Watson, but the similarity was there, just begging to be pointed out."

"And do you not also earn your bread and cheese by helping the victims of such crimes?"

"I do," he admitted.

"And since I have never known you to go hungry, save by choice, can I assume that the remuneration for your work, when you choose to take it, is quite substantial?"

"Well-played, Watson! Well-played."

"You know, Holmes, there are some things that are simply better left unsaid." However, I did have to admit that there was a certain element of truth in his words, and I had never looked at my literary endeavors from quite that point of view. Still, his words had nettled me, but I felt that I had given as good as I had got in that exchange.

Deciding to change the subject, I said, "Do you think Dell'Osso's information is valid?"

"He has no reason to lie, and if he is telling the truth, it will move us one step closer to our quarry. Tomorrow, I shall look into his allegations, but for the moment, one more pipe before bed, I think."

The next morning Holmes and I breakfasted together and he departed as soon as he had finished. I spent much of the day writing and ate my lunch alone. I was beginning to wonder how Holmes was faring with his inquiries when I heard his familiar tread on the stairs.

When he entered the room, I could tell from his expression that he had made some progress, and I knew that he would tell me about it in his own time. After a while, he looked at me and grinned, "So it's like that, is it?"

"I assume you will tell me about your day when you are ready – and not before."

Throwing up his hands, he laughed and said, "Another round to the good Doctor. I must say, today proved quite interesting."

"Oh?"

"Yes, I visited no less than four men on the list provided by my friend, and none of them was wearing a signet although two did have rather distinctive watch fobs but neither would be mistaken for the one described by Dell'Osso.

"And that is progress?"

"Of a sort. We have winnowed the list from 10 suspects to six," he said. "I then stopped by the British Museum to visit Dr. Smith. The exhibit is now scheduled to open in three weeks. The museum is planning to make a formal announcement tomorrow."

"And the Tara Brooch?"

"It is to be one of the centerpieces of the exhibit."

"And do you really think, this Merchant of Menace, as I have decided to dub him, will be audacious enough to attempt a theft under the newly improved safety measures that have been implemented?"

"The Merchant of Menace? You outdo yourself, Watson. As to his attempting to procure the Tara Brooch, I am rather counting on it," said my friend. "Scotland Yard has been tasked with providing round-the-clock security. There will be two uniformed officers standing guard over the brooch at all times. During the day, two CID men also will be on hand in the gallery and, one hopes, rather less conspicuous. At night, two other constables will keep watch over the display case."

"You make it sound as though it will be impossible to steal," I remarked.

"One can but erect impediments, Watson. Even so, I still have certain reservations about the brooch. Remember, we are dealing here with a very clever and resourceful thief who will stop at nothing to obtain what he wants."

"Holmes, you have bested many criminals, including the late, unlamented Professor Moriarty. I am certain you are doing all that may be done."

"Thank you, Watson. And now what has Mrs. Hudson prepared for dinner?"

After we had devoured a savory ham pie, Holmes went out again, so I spent the evening reading and beginning to transcribe the notes from an incident I had decided to title "The Adventure of the Bowed Bookshelf."

When Holmes returned shortly after nine, there was an undeniable jauntiness about him, so I observed, "You certainly look pleased with yourself."

"I am rather," he replied.

"And the occasion of your good spirits?"

"Before we discuss my evening, let me ask, how are you getting on with that bookshelf adventure?"

Although I should have been used to that sort of thing from Holmes, I was taken aback in spite of myself by my friend's unerring observation. "Confound it, Holmes! How could you possibly know how I spent my evening?"

"Your right cuff is stained with ink, which tells me that you have been writing."

"That's an easy observation," I replied. "How could you know which adventure I have been working on? I have several that are as yet untouched and this is my first attempt at that particular case."

"That is the easiest part of all," replied Holmes. "Your bookshelves are usually a study in organization. Yet tonight, several volumes are residing in places where they would not normally be found. In an effort to recreate the scene, you have moved them about, and as far as I can recall, we have had only one case of late involving a bookshelf of any kind."

"But I moved those yesterday," I countered.

"Yes, but your cuff has not been near your inkwell until tonight," he laughed.

"Enough of my night," I said. "Tell me about your evening."

Pulling a small parcel from the pocket of his greatcoat, he replied, "I have just recovered 'The First Book of Urizen' for Lady Darbent."

"My word, Holmes. How on Earth did you manage that?"

"I am, if nothing else, Watson, dogged in my persistence – a term I believe you have used to describe my efforts on one or two occasions in your literary endeavors.

"As you know, I was working my way through the list provided by my friend. As it turned out, the second call I made tonight was to the man who until just recently possessed the book."

Before he would tell me anything else, Holmes forbade me from revealing the buyer's name or providing even the slightest clue to his identity. I was forced to agree although I will admit I did so rather grudgingly.

"Upon being ushered into his study, where I was kept waiting for several minutes, I thought he might be the culprit given the various *objets d'art* that graced that room, including a Rembrandt that went missing in the 18th century, a Vermeer I know to be of uncertain provenance and a Reynolds that I believe was stolen from its owner's home several years ago.

When he finally entered, I saw the telltale watch fob and ring immediately.

"He began by telling me how busy he was and how I should consider myself fortunate that he was making time for me at all. Finally, he said, 'I will give you exactly two minutes, Mr. Holmes. That is all the time I can spare.'

"I replied, 'Sir, you can either make time for me or the police. The choice is yours.' You may be certain that captured his attention. I pointed out the Vermeer and the Rembrandt, saving the Reynolds for last. 'You may have acquired one of these legally, perhaps even two, although I am rather doubtful. However, to have three pieces, all gone missing under mysterious circumstances, beggars the imagination. So I suggest you either make a bit more time for me or clear your calendar for my friend, Inspector Lestrade.'

"'What is it that you want?' he asked.

"'I want two things,' I replied.

"'I knew it,' he exclaimed. 'You're nothing more than a common blackmailer.'"

"'I have no interest in your money. Rather, I want you to give me 'The First Book of Urizen' so that I may return it to its rightful owner and then I would appreciate it greatly if you were to tell me about the person from whom you obtained the book. And before you bluster and proclaim you do not have the book, I want you to remember that I can have the police here in short order.' With that I held up an officer's whistle."

"And how did he respond to that?" I asked.

"Surprisingly, he acquiesced immediately. I suspect had Scotland Yard been summoned, a search of the house and his other properties might well have turned up a number of other items that should properly be residing someplace else."

"But to give in that quickly?"

"I think you have to understand the mind of a collector. He gathers things because he admires them – and he likes nothing more than showing off his acquisitions. With the publicity surrounding the theft of 'The Book of Urizen,' he might not be able to share that particular beauty with anyone but his closest friends for several years – possibly longer. I also assured him that when I captured the man who had sold him the book, I would extend every effort to make certain that he recovered whatever he had paid for the book."

"And was his information about the man who sold him the book useful?"

"Not terribly, I am afraid. He admitted that he had let it be known for several years that he would be willing to pay handsomely for a copy of 'The Book of Urizen.' He said that he was finally approached at a party more than a year ago by a man who told him that he might be able to procure a copy of the book in question. After a bit of haggling, a price was agreed upon and three months later, he received a note informing him that a copy of the book had been procured from a collector in Wales. They met, and he then took the book and had its authenticity verified by Dell'Osso after which he paid the seller. He claims he and the man have not seen nor communicated with each other since."

"Could he describe the man?"

"He could add nothing to what we already know. Dark beard, tinted glasses, perhaps six feet tall."

"So aside from recovering Lady Darbent's book, which is no mean feat, you have made little actual progress in your pursuit of the Merchant."

"I would not go that far, Watson. I have confirmed what I suspected: That our quarry is a meticulous planner, and that he is extremely patient. Consider the length of time between his first meeting and the actual sale of the book. Given his presence at the same party as the buyer, we also know that he can move in the rarefied social circles of British society. No Watson, we are making slow but steady headway, and we do have other irons in the fire."

"Do we?" I asked.

"Indeed! I am approaching this particular problem from a number of different angles. Certainly one of my several vantage points will afford me the necessary insight to bring this man to justice."

"That's all well and good," I replied, "but I feel as though we should be doing something."

"We are doing something, old friend. We are biding our time. This is not a case where we can press on willy-nilly; rather, it is one where we must bait our hooks and sit patiently hoping that our enticement is attractive to the fish in question."

"The Brooch of Tara," I exclaimed.

"What of it?" asked Holmes.

"That's your bait," I replied. "I know it."

"Old friend, do you really think I would put at risk one of the national treasures of Ireland and possibly jeopardize relations between Britain and Eire merely to solve a case?"

I must admit that Holmes' remark did give me pause; nevertheless, I thought I detected just the hint of a smile on his face before he turned away.

Chapter 7

As Holmes had promised, the British Museum announced the upcoming exhibition the next day. The press had obviously been given advance notice as there was a lengthy story about the "Gold of the Gaels" in The Times that morning.

Had I not had an interest in the exhibit already, I would certainly have made plans to see it as the article detailed the history of a number of items, including the Cross of Cong, the Cloth of Gold Vestments of Waterford, the Ardagh Chalice and, of course, the Tara Brooch. I was particularly taken with the Ardagh Chalice, which had been discovered just a few decades earlier in 1868 by two young men who were digging potatoes. Although the chalice presumably dated from around the eighth century, it had remained buried all those hundreds of years until those two men had accidentally unearthed it.

Equally fascinating was the story of the Tara Brooch. According to the report, the brooch, another recent discovery, was found in 1850 on the beach at Bettystown, near Laytown, County Meath, some 30 miles north of Dublin and about 15 miles from Tara. The finder, a peasant woman, claimed to have come across it in a box she saw partially buried in the sand. The brooch was then sold to a dealer and then subsequently resold to G.&S. Waterhouse, a Dublin jewelry firm. At the time, the Celtic Revival was very much in vogue and the piece was renamed the Tara Brooch, after the Hill of Tara, traditionally seen as the seat of the High Kings of Ireland. Apparently, this was done in order to increase its appeal to the public.

As I sat there pondering these two unlikely discoveries, my mind began to wander. Holmes interrupted my thoughts by remarking, "It is indeed curious how myths are made is it not, my friend?"

"Blast it all, Holmes! How could you possibly know what I have been thinking?"

"Following your train of thought was rather simple, old friend. When I walked by a few minutes ago, I noticed you were reading the article about the upcoming exhibit. I watched as you perused the article and then returned to reread several sections. Although you have obviously finished the article, the paper has remained open to that same page for some three minutes now, without you so much as glancing at it.

"During that time, it was quite obvious that you were considering what you had just read. However, after a moment or two, your gaze shifted, albeit ever so briefly, to your well-worn copy of Malory's *Le Morte d'Arthur,* which enjoys a pride of place among your books. It is no great stretch to watch your mind at work as you considered the relative merits of the legendary figures of Camelot and the story of the Tara Brooch."

"Had you lived in King Arthur's time, they would have either burned you at the stake as a sorcerer, or Merlin might have had to do you in."

"Perhaps," Holmes replied, "but we live in the here and now, and the man we seek is no myth although he is quite an accomplished thief."

"And you think he will attempt to steal the Tara Brooch?"

"I rather think he will have someone do it for him, and that is both a blessing and a curse."

"Why do you say that?"

"It is a blessing because, if he holds true to form, the person he employs will not be a professional thief, but that fact complicates things because it could be anyone entering the museum. It might even be someone we know."

"You can't be serious!" I exclaimed.

"With the right encouragement, I think even you could be coerced into the attempting the theft," replied Holmes.

"I rather doubt that," I said.

"Suppose, a stranger accosted you on the street and said, 'If you do not steal the Tara Brooch for me, both Sherlock Holmes and Mrs. Hudson will die agonizing deaths. Now, go to the museum and return with the brooch.'

"What would you do?"

I must confess it had never occurred to me that I might find myself on the horns of such of a terrible dilemma. Reluctantly, I had to admit Holmes was correct and given that choice, I would do everything in my power to make certain that he and Mrs. Hudson came to no harm.

"And there you have it, Watson. Once you have discovered a man's or a woman's Achilles' heel, you simply apply the appropriate pressure, and that person can be made to do your bidding."

"You make it all sound so cold and calculated," I remarked.

"That is precisely because his actions are both cold and calculated. You have often described me as a thinking machine, an automaton, devoid of emotion."

"I was merely taking poetic license," I said in my own defense.

"Be that as it may, there is a certain truth in your description of me. Logic and reason, devoid of emotion, are my stock in trade. However, I choose to use my powers for good. Our foe has chosen an entirely different path, and that is why this man must be stopped. He preys upon people's nobler instincts – preserving a loved one, for instance – to force them to carry out his nefarious plans. As you know, I am not a religious man, but I do believe I know evil when I encounter it."

At that moment, I heard the bell ring. A minute or two later, Mrs. Hudson knocked on the door. Before she could enter, Holmes bellowed, "Just show Inspector Lestrade up, if you would Mrs. Hudson."

"Right away, Mr. Holmes," she replied without entering.

"How on Earth could you know that it is Lestrade is at the door?"

"I have been expecting him," replied Holmes, glancing at his watch. "And he is running a bit late."

At that moment Lestrade entered our room. Holmes rose and looked at the police officer and then stated, "Your superiors are breathing down your neck?"

Lestrade was so used to Holmes' pronouncements of this nature that he was not even the least bit startled.

"They are indeed, Mr. Holmes, and Lord Thornton continues to make my life miserable," replied Lestrade. "I have tried explaining to him that we are working on recovering his knife, by he wants immediate results. I don't understand why you couldn't have taken the case."

"In point of fact, I have taken the case, Lestrade, but I have chosen to keep him in the dark about my involvement for the exact reason you just enumerated.

"As an absolute last resort, you may tell him that I have involved myself again and am doing everything in my power to return his *jambiya* to him, but emphasize to him that if he insists upon continually inserting himself into the investigation, he is doing little more than aiding and abetting the thief. You might also insinuate that his continued interference could cause me to look deeper into the provenance of the *jambiya*."

"Should it become necessary, I will relay your message," said Lestrade gratefully. "However, even with your reputation, I am afraid I don't see it doing much good."

"Tell him if my word is not sufficient, he may call upon me at Baker Street to discuss the matter further. Now, to the business at hand. Have you obtained what I asked for, Lestrade?"

Pulling a paper from his inside breast pocket, he handed it to Holmes. "I have no idea why you want this Mr. Holmes, and, truth be told, I'm not certain I want to know. But here it is, and as you know, it must be kept confidential."

"Inspector, I give you my word, your secret is safe with me."

"You have never let me down, Mr. Holmes, so I am going to take you at your word. Now, I must be on my way, it seems a number of shop windows were broken in the Elephant and Castle section last night, and a young man was stabbed to death."

"Look to the gangs, Lestrade. It has come to my attention that a power struggle has erupted within the Forty Thieves."

"Thank you, Mr. Holmes. I had heard much the same thing."

After the Inspector had departed, I asked Holmes, "Would you be betraying a confidence if I were to ask what Lestrade had given you?"

"Not at all, Watson." Holding the paper up, Holmes said, "These are the instructions and the timetable for transporting the 'Gold of the Gaels' artifacts from Dublin to London."

"Are you planning to go to Ireland and accompany them here?"

"Not at all. I have something totally different in mind. It just remains to be seen whether or not the powers that be are still willing to cooperate or are wavering."

Over the next week or so, Holmes was a veritable whirlwind of activity. I know that he visited Dr. Smith at the museum on a number of occasions as well as calling upon Lestrade several times.

Finally, two days before the exhibit was to open, Holmes said to me over breakfast, "The 'Gold of the Gaels' artifacts are scheduled to arrive at Euston on a special train due in around noon. I promised Lestrade I would meet him at the station. Would you care to join us?"

"I most certainly would," I exclaimed. And so it was that shortly before noon, we joined Dr. Smith, Inspector Lestrade and a contingent of no fewer than 10 uniformed officers on a platform at Euston. We had been waiting only a very few minutes when the hissing of brakes told us that the train was pulling into the station. The special consisted of the locomotive, two freight cars and a single passenger car in the rear.

When the doors of the freight car doors were opened, I saw that both cars were loaded with wooden crates, all of which had "British Museum" stenciled in large letters on them. Inside each car were stationed four armed guards. They were a fearsome looking bunch. Armed to the teeth, they all carried rifles and some had side arms visible as well. A number of them sported beards and moustaches, and truth be told, they looked more like a gang of desperadoes from the American Wild West than a top-notch phalanx of security guards.

Suddenly, a dapper-looking man in a perfectly tailored tweed suit stepped from the single passenger car. He headed directly for Dr. Smith and said, "Dr. Smith, it is so good to see you again. The trip was made entirely without incident." Smith then introduced us to Charles Dowd, the director of the National Museum of Ireland.

As pleasantries were being exchanged, the officers loaded the crates onto dollies, which in turn were loaded onto wagons for transport to the British Museum. All of this was done under the watchful eyes of the security guards and constables as well as Holmes and Lestrade.

Dr. Smith, Dowd, Holmes, Lestrade and I then proceeded outside where Smith and Dowd boarded a hansom and Lestrade, Holmes and I followed in a growler. As we rode to the museum, Lestrade observed, "Everything seems to have gone fairly smoothly thus far, wouldn't you say, Mr. Holmes?"

My friend merely smiled and said, "Well there were certainly enough guards."

When we arrived at the museum, we rejoined Smith and Dowd, the former of whom then ushered us into the renovated display hall that would house the "Gold of the Gaels" exhibit.

"As you can see," Smith began, pointing to the barred windows and special display cases, "we have taken every possible precaution in terms of security."

While he was speaking, museum workers were bringing in the various crates on trundlers and dollies. At that point, we were joined by Dr. Dennis Lamb, the head of the museum. Looking at Smith, he asked, "I assume everything arrived safe and sound?"

"We will find out shortly," said Smith. "The workers are just beginning to open the crates now."

At that point, a museum guard entered the room. Coming directly to Holmes, he said, "There is a woman who insists upon seeing you, Mr. Holmes."

My friend looked at Smith, who nodded, and then Holmes said, "Please escort her to Dr. Smith's office and inform her that we shall join her momentarily."

At that point, Dr. Lamb said, "I must say, I have been looking forward to examining these pieces. My mother is Irish, and she is quite excited about the exhibit, especially the Tara Brooch."

"It is a magnificent piece," said Dowd. Pointing to a small crate, he said, I believe it is packed in that box. He then turned to one of the workers and said, "Please bring that one here." Pulling a piece of paper from the inside pocket of his jacket, Dowd consulted it and then he looked at the box. "Yes, that is No. 54," he said pointing to the numbers stenciled on the box. Turning to the workman, he said, "Please open it."

After he had pried off the top, the workman stepped back. Dowd then stepped forward and plunging his hands into the wood wool that filled the crate, he produced a small wooden box. It was constructed of some sort of dark-colored hardwood and Gaelic symbols had been carved into its lid. Placing it in the display case that Smith had earlier indicated was reserved for the Tara Brooch, he threw up the lid, turned to face us and said proudly, "Gentlemen, I give you the Tara Brooch, one of Ireland's greatest treasures."

Looking at the box, all I saw was a single sheet of white paper laying on the green velvet lining. The sheet had been folded in half. When none of us reacted, Dowd turned to the box and exclaimed, "What is this?"

Grasping the paper, he opened it. His face turned ashen, and he gestured toward Holmes. Almost choking on his words, he said, "I believe this is intended for you, Mr. Holmes."

Taking the paper, Holmes glanced at it, and a slight smile played across his face.

"What does it say?" bellowed Lestrade.

"Read it, Inspector," replied my friend, passing him the paper.

After glancing at it, Lestrade's only response was "Blimey!"

"Lestrade," I said, and he then handed me the sheet. In the middle of the page were two lines in a graceful cursive. One line was above the fold and the other below. The message was short but succinct:

"To borrow a phrase,

'Dear me, Mr. Holmes. Dear me!'"

Looking at me, Holmes remarked, "Well, Watson, it would appear that you draw your readers from all walks of life as well as both sides of the law."

Chapter 8

To say that confusion reigned in the gallery for the next few minutes would be a gross understatement. Dowd was loudly reproaching Dr. Smith, "I knew that sending the brooch here was a mistake," while Lestrade was bellowing orders to the museum workers and the guards to seal all the entrances.

After a minute or two, Holmes said to Lestrade, "I rather think the horse has left the barn, don't you, Inspector?" As you might expect, my friend had somehow managed to retain his equanimity despite all the bewilderment surrounding him, a fact I believe Lestrade and the others found more than a little off-putting.

When there was finally a brief lull in the recriminations, Holmes said to all the principals, "I think it best if we adjourn to Dr. Smith's office. I have someone there I should like you to meet."

Although the walk to Smith's office could not have lasted more than four or five minutes, it seemed like a death march. The only person not totally disconsolate was Holmes. When we reached Smith's office, which had undergone a sea change and was now the picture of organization and tidiness, we found an attractive woman sitting in the waiting room. She rose when we entered and I could see that she was of average height, with brown hair. Still, there was an unmistakable force about her personality. She was wearing a rather fashionable gray dress that had obviously been designed for her, a small hat and a patterned gray scarf that contrasted neatly with the darker hue of her outfit.

"Gentleman, I should like to introduce Madame Isabella Cocilovo-Kozzi. She is an antiquarian with a special affinity for the printed word." Looking at Smith, he added, "I am sure you have passed her shop in Bedford Square on a number of occasions."

"Indeed, I have," said Smith. "It is a pleasure to meet you."

"And I you," she replied, shaking his hand.

"Mr. Holmes, I don't mean to interfere with your social engagement," said Dowd acidly. "I just want to remind you that one of Ireland's national treasures has been stolen, and while we are standing here exchanging pleasantries, the thief is no doubt making plans to dispose of his ill-gotten gains."

Holmes looked at Dowd and said, "Sir, I can assure you that we have things well in hand, and you have nothing to worry about."

"How can you say that when the brooch is gone?" he blustered.

Then turning to Smith, he said, "I am truly sorry, but I cannot put any of the other treasures at risk. I am afraid the exhibit will have to be canceled. All your security improvements failed to protect the brooch, so I fear I must doubt their efficacy in safeguarding the other artifacts."

"See here, Mr. Dowd," began Lestrade, "I don't think you can blame the museum's security. The brooch appears to have been stolen before it ever arrived in London,"

"I quite agree with Inspector Lestrade," added Holmes. "You accompanied the brooch from the National Museum of Ireland to the train, did you not?"

Dowd nodded emphatically as Holmes continued, "And I assume you rode in the freight car with the crates?"

"Come now, Mr. Holmes, you can't expect me to sit up all night like a watchman. That is why we hired the extra guards."

"So then I can safely assume that you did not make the voyage across the Irish Sea in the hold of the ship? I can also assume that on the trip to London, you rode in the passenger car? The fact is, Mr. Dowd, the crate containing the brooch appears to have been more often out of your sight than in it during its journey here!"

"What are you suggesting?" roared Dowd.

"I am not suggesting anything; I am merely pointing out the obvious."

"You're not going to hang this on me," he bellowed.

"There is nothing to hang," replied Holmes. Turning to Madame Cocilovo-Kozzi, Holmes said, "Madam, if you would be so kind."

She then removed the scarf from her neck, unclasped a piece of jewelry that had been concealed beneath and handed it to Holmes. Turning around, Holmes then repeated the exact words that Dowd had uttered a few minutes earlier: "Gentlemen, I give you the Tara Brooch, one of Ireland's greatest treasures."

Words could never do justice were I to attempt to describe the look of sheer amazement on the faces of Dowd and Lestrade.

Taking the piece and examining it, Dowd could only wonder aloud, "How is this possible?"

Lestrade showed a bit more *savoir faire* in that instance and simply looked at my friend and said, "Well done, Mr. Holmes. I suppose I should be cross, but under the circumstances, I think your little ploy can be forgiven."

Turning to Smith, Dowd asked, "Were you in on this?"

"I am afraid, I rather twisted Dr. Smith's arm in that respect," interjected Holmes. "Given the previous attempts to steal the Tara Brooch, I suspected another endeavor would be undertaken to liberate the brooch from its rightful owners. With new security guards and a lengthy journey, it seemed to me the timing could not be more propitious for such a task.

"To that end, I had Dr. Smith contact the director of the National Museum, George Tindall Plunkett, and explain my fears and outline my plans. He readily agreed, so about two weeks before the exhibit was to be packed, a replacement brooch, which was constructed under the supervision of Dr. Smith, was taken to Ireland by Madame Cocilovo-Kozzi and substituted for the original.

"She then returned to England where she has kept the Tara Brooch in her safe until today when she brought it here to the museum."

"But why was I not told?" insisted Dowd.

"Mr. Dowd, I think you would agree that the best way to keep a secret is by limiting those who know about it. Because you suspected nothing was amiss, you played your part perfectly. You strike me as a forthright man, and I can tell that you are not used to dissembling.

"Had you known of my plan, I am certain that you would have acted differently, and I believe that might have alerted our adversary. As for Dr. Smith, he knew only of the substitution and was kept in the dark about all the other particulars. The same can be said of Mr. Plunkett. The only ones who knew the plan in its entirety were Madame Cocilovo-Kozzi and myself."

At that point, Dr. Smith said, "Mr. Holmes, I know that I owe you a debt of gratitude, and I am certain that Mr. Dowd feels the same way."

Having had a moment to collect himself while Holmes was speaking, Dowd then said, "I apologize, Mr. Holmes. No one likes being kept in the dark, but given what has transpired, I cannot argue with your methods nor your results."

He and Holmes then shook hands. Dowd then turned to Smith and said, "Let's get this in that new-fangled display case, where I hope it will remain safe and sound."

"I will accompany you," said Lestrade.

As they reached the door that led to Smith's waiting room, Dowd turned back to Holmes and asked, "Since we have the original. Who has the copy and how did they get it?"

"I cannot tell you who has the copy," Holmes said, "not yet at any rate. As for the thief, consider, what is the only new element in this entire picture?"

"The guards," I exclaimed.

"Bravo, Watson. Were I you, Mr. Dowd, I should have Inspector Lestrade bring all eight guards down to Scotland Yard where he can thoroughly check their identities and make certain they are exactly who they say they are."

"I was planning to do that very thing," said Lestrade.

After they had departed, Holmes turned to Madame Cocilovo-Kozzi and said, "You have handled yourself like a true professional."

Smiling at him, she then asked, "Can I assume that we are now even once again and the slate has been wiped clean?"

"Indeed," said Holmes.

She then bid us both a pleasant afternoon and left the museum.

As we walked out, I turned to Holmes and said, "It is quite fortunate that I am familiar with your methods; otherwise, I should be as offended as Dowd."

"There are no secrets between us, old friend. Occasionally, however, a little mendacity may be the only means of reaching my goal."

"So then, like Machiavelli, you do believe that the ends justify the means?"

"From time to time," laughed Holmes.

After dinner that night, Mrs. Hudson delivered a telegram from Lestrade. It said simply. "Two guards missing. Stop. The search is on. Stop. Lestrade."

Holmes showed me the wire and a moment later, Mrs. Hudson knocked on the door a second time. Holmes bade her enter, and our landlady said, "I'm terribly sorry, Mr. Holmes, but I found this envelope addressed to you slipped under the front door. It must have arrived while you were out. I slipped it into my apron pocket and quite forgot about it until just now."

Handing the envelope to Holmes, she curtseyed and closed the door behind her.

"What can this be?" I asked.

"There is only one way to find out," said my friend. Taking a letter opener, he slit the envelope, and removed a single sheet of white paper. On it in a cursive that I recognized was a brief note:

"Well-played Mr. Holmes.

I'm certain our paths will cross again."

Chapter 9

Never one to rest on his laurels, Holmes began making inquiries about the missing guards the next morning. However, his efforts proved fruitless. He learned the two bogus security men had joined the other six at the National Museum of Ireland in Dublin. They had presented proper identification as well as all the necessary paperwork. They told their fellow guards that at the last minute the home office had decided to assign two extra men as a precaution, and they had just missed joining the other guards on their ship across the Atlantic.

Lestrade sent us a note the next day. Holmes asked that I read it to him so he could concentrate. "Lestrade says little more has been learned. He says the missing men have been identified as Henry Dearborn and Edward Bates."

Upon hearing the names, Holmes laughed out loud. "I must admit this Merchant fellow is a bit cheeky," he observed.

"Why do you say that?" I asked.

"Henry Dearborn served as Secretary of War to Thomas Jefferson while Edward Bates filled the position of Attorney General in President Lincoln's Cabinet. A broader knowledge of American history on someone's part might have prevented this theft," he observed drily.

Although he turned to his many and varied sources throughout London over the next few weeks, there was nothing in the way of information about the two men.

Eventually, our lives returned to their daily routines. Although constantly busy with other cases, Holmes devoted what little free time he had to making inquiries about the man even he had come to call "the Merchant."

One morning while he was perusing the papers, I heard him say, "Is it possible?"

"Is what possible, old chap?"

"I see that the Louvre has just received a considerable donation for its collection of Islamic art. I was wondering whether our Merchant might have been approached by someone wishing to acquire one or more of those attractive objects."

"I would assume that there is a buyer of some sort for all types of art," I observed.

"Well-said, Watson. *De gustibus non est disputendam.* Perhaps we can create a market for one of the pieces in the collection."

"That might work, Holmes."

My friend then set about researching Islamic art and after a few days during which he eschewed both sustenance and sleep in favor of reading and planning, he announced, "I think I have it, Watson. While there are several items which our quarry might find infinitely attractive, I believe the Baptistère de St. Louis might prove too enticing too resist."

"I'm afraid I must plead ignorance with regard to that particular piece," I admitted.

"The Baptistère de St. Louis is a metal basin crafted by an artisan named Mohammed ibn al-Zain sometime in the early-14th century. Although the basin is made primarily of hammered bronze, it has also been inlaid with gold, silver, and niello.

"In truth, the Baptistère de St. Louis is actually a bit of a misnomer," he continued. "It wasn't until the 18th century that the basin received its name. And while it was used as the baptismal font for several royal children, including Louis XIII, the vessel did not exist during the time of Louis IX, who died in 1270 and was canonized a few decades later."

"It certainly sounds like something that might pique the Merchant's interest," I said, "and I'm equally certain it would fetch a pretty penny from a serious collector."

Holmes had decided to write to the Louvre, but before he could compose his letter, Lestrade paid us a visit. "I am still amazed that you anticipated the theft of the brooch, Mr. Holmes, and I can assure you that the powers that be are equally grateful."

"Thank you, Inspector, but I am certain you did not journey all this way just to convey some vague expressions of gratitude from your superiors."

"True enough, Mr. Holmes. I understand that you have been searching high and low for the missing guards," he began, "and I believe we may have located one."

The change in Holmes was immediate. Suddenly, he was like a prize hound straining to be let off the leash. "And where is he now?" asked my friend.

"In a Paris morgue. It seems a body carrying identification in the name of Edward Bates was pulled from the Seine near the Pont Neuf on the Left Bank," reported Lestrade. "He had nothing on his person but his wallet. There was no money nor anything else in his pockets."

"And how did he end up in the Seine?" asked Holmes.

"He appears to have been stabbed to death. I have asked a friend of mine on the Surete to ship the body here. I thought you might want to examine it."

"How did the Surete come to learn of your interest in Mr. Bates?" asked Holmes.

"I provided detailed descriptions of both missing guards to a number of international law enforcement agencies, including the Irish Royal Constabulary, the officials in several German states, and, of course, the Surete."

"You outdo yourself, Lestrade. When is it expected to arrive?"

"Barring the unforeseen, you should be able to see it at the morgue either late tonight or early tomorrow."

"Capital," exclaimed Holmes. "Please wire me the minute I may examine the corpse."

After he had left, Holmes looked at me said, "You know what this development means?"

"I don't want to appear naïve, so please enlighten me."

"Think, Watson. Two guards are missing and one ends up dead in the Seine. And as we were discussing earlier, the Louvre has just received a consignment of priceless Islamic art."

"The other one killed him!" I exclaimed, and Holmes nodded. "So that other guard was actually the Merchant?"

"Bravo, like Lestrade, you outdo yourself."

"So we have seen the Merchant. Now we know what he looks like."

"Let us not jump to that conclusion just yet. I will concede that we were, in all likelihood, in the presence of the Merchant, but I am equally certain that he took proper pains to disguise his true appearance.

"Both men, if you remember, were bearded, and while I noticed it at the time, I thought little of it. If you recall, however, the one we now believe to be the Merchant took considerable pains to remain in the rear at all times. Something I noted but failed to ascertain the true meaning of at the time."

"But he was on the scene," I continued.

"Yes, he and his partner were obviously the ones who made off with the fake brooch and left the note in its place."

"So why did he kill his partner?"

"I can only speculate on that," said Holmes. "They may have had a falling out or perhaps the Merchant decided that his cohort was now dispensable. We can only assume the dead man came to be looked upon as a loose end, a liability. He may have learned of the Merchant's past endeavors, which raises the possibility of blackmail. We can speculate all day, but until we have facts and data, our musings are meaningless."

"I understand that our quarry had decided to eliminate the possibility, but why wait? And why kill him in France?"

"Unless I am very much mistaken," Holmes said, "He needed his confederate to help him execute his planned theft at the Louvre. Once everything was in place, he then became expendable."

"So you think, the Merchant may have already stolen the Baptistère?"

"If not that, then something else equally rare and valuable."

"Still, if the dead man knew him, then others must know him as well."

"Indeed, the problem is we have but a vague description and an alias. Moreover, I am certain that he has taken pains to alter his appearance once again and to assume a new identity by now."

"So what's to be done?"

"We examine the corpse and hope and for the best, but at the same time, we prepare for the worst."

The wire from Lestrade arrived shortly after nine that evening, and a few moments later, Holmes and I were in a cab headed for the Kew Mortuary. Located just east of Kew Bridge on Greyhound Lane, the small building was often used as a temporary resting place for bodies pulled from the Thames.

When we arrived, Lestrade was waiting for us outside. "I had the corpse brought here for obvious reasons," he said, nodding toward the nearby river.

"Well done, Lestrade. Let us see if the body can tell us anything."

We entered the small building, where an officer was standing guard. "There's really not much to see," said Lestrade."

"Oh, you might be surprised at the tales dead men do tell," remarked my friend.

Pulling back the sheet to the man's waist, Holmes began to carefully examine the face, looking first at the eyes and then the teeth. He then turned his attention to a tattoo on the man's right bicep. "Are there any other tattoos?" he asked.

"Just the one," said Lestrade.

"What do you make of it?" he asked the two of us.

"It looks rather like a 'Y' in a circle," I observed.

"And so it does," agreed Lestrade.

Looking at Lestrade, Holmes remarked, "I must admit to having an advantage over you, for, as Watson will attest, I am currently at work on a monograph about tattoos.

"That 'Y' that you see is supposed to represent the Chicago River. At Wolf's Point in that city, the river divides into two branches, the North and the South. If you look closely, you can see that the border in the circle around the 'Y' is actually intended to represent a series of small waves. I think we can safely conclude that our Mr. Bates, though I rather doubt that was his real name, hailed from Chicago."

"My word, Holmes."

"Lestrade, where are his effects?"

The Inspector signaled to the officer who placed a wire basket filled with clothing on the table next to the body.

Holmes turned his lens on the various articles of clothing, beginning with the jacket, then the shirt and trousers and finally the belt and the shoes. "I should say these garments certainly proves he was an American. Although the labels have been removed, the workmanship is most definitely American, and the boots could have only been made in that country."

"So what do we have, Mr. Holmes?" asked Lestrade.

"Not a great deal, I'm afraid. The tattoo is most telling, but the clothing has yielded nothing significant. I shall make inquiries, Inspector, and you do the same. Although I am not optimistic, we can compare notes in a few weeks."

"Will do, Mr. Holmes."

"And Lestrade, thank you for allowing me to examine the body."

"Think nothing of it, Mr. Holmes. As you might suspect, I had an ulterior motive."

Holmes was busy the next morning, composing several cables, and then waiting – never one of my friend's strong suits – for replies.

As each of the return cables arrived, Holmes would peruse it three and four times and then throw it on the table in disgust.

"It is as I feared, Watson. The only promising lead, the tattoo, has led us nowhere. That particular symbol has only gained a degree of prominence in the last decade after it was selected as the winning design in a contest sponsored by a newspaper in that city. Both the original, which you saw on the body, and an inverted version were quickly embraced by members of that city's underworld as a sort of badge of belonging."

"So we are no further along than we were before?"

"We have made a few minimal gains. I think we can say with a degree of certainty our quarry is American, either that or he is an actor of no small repute."

"Much like yourself," I ventured, hoping to lighten the mood.

"Indeed," said Holmes, taking my words as a compliment.

"But why do you say that?"

"Consider, neither Mrs. Sweeney nor the man who purchased 'The Book of Urizen' mentioned anything about an American accent. And I should think that would have been something rather obvious about the man."

"True enough," I said. "But why couldn't he be an Englishman posing as an American."

"That is certainly a possibility, and one I had considered, but he needed a trusted accomplice to help him steal the brooch. I am certain that when he learned the museum had retained an American firm to guard the exhibit during the journey from Ireland to London, he saw that as the hand of Providence beckoning to him.

"So he recruited someone he knew, someone he trusted and that someone was an American. No, Watson, you are correct. He could be any English-speaking nationality, but as a working hypothesis, let us posit for the moment that he is an American."

I suggested, "Perhaps the question you need to consider is: Why did the museum hire an American firm in the first place?"

"I have looked into that. The Pinkerton Agency, which is most reputable, has been trying to make inroads in Europe, and its board had offered their services to several museums *gratis* a few years ago in return for testimonials and endorsements. No one had ever taken them up on their offer – until recently.

"You may remember that Mr. Douglas of Birlstone Manor had served with the Pinkertons with distinction. No, Watson. The agency is above reproach, but like any such group, it can be infiltrated, and I am certain the Pinkertons have their share of bad apples. That is a line of inquiry I am continuing to pursue although I must admit I have scant hope of it coming to fruition."

"So then what is our course of action?"

"Unless one of my many inquiries takes root, we must once again wait and remain vigilant. There are too many precious objects to even begin considering what his next target might be. I believe Langland in Piers Plowman says that 'Patience is a virtue.'"

He was of course merely rehashing the old Latin proverb, *maxima enim, patientia virtus*, which tells us that patience is the greatest virtue.

"No, old friend. The first act of this drama has concluded. We can only wait in the wings and hope to be called back onto the stage in the second act."

"Holmes, I have seldom heard this kind of pessimism from you."

"It is not pessimism at all, my friend. It is realism. At the moment, our adversary has the lead role. He is the protagonist, and we can only react, should he choose to act again – and I have no doubt that he will. That is why I say, we must remain vigilant. In the meantime, we have other business to which we must attend. Inspector Hopkins sent me a wire yesterday asking for my help with a particularly nasty bit of business at the Blackwell Buildings in the East End. That is a case where I can be of service, so to that I will turn my attention."

However, after sitting in his chair for a few moments, Holmes suddenly sat bolt upright and asked: "But why leave the identification on the body?"

"I'm not certain that I follow you…"

"Your Merchant could have dispatched his accomplice anywhere and hidden the body. However, the corpse turns up in the Seine, and from what we can gather there was no attempt made to weigh down the body and thus conceal it. Rather, he left the bogus identification papers in the pockets for us to find and nothing else. So, I repeat: Why?"

"Obviously, as you have said, there is something there that interests him. Perhaps he is planning to steal something else."

"Or perhaps, as I am now more inclined to think, he has stolen it already. And this is his way of summoning us to witness his handiwork. Watson, I think a short excursion to Paris is most definitely in order."

Chapter 10

And so it was that several hours later, Holmes and I were gazing at the White Cliffs of Dover in the distance behind us as we prepared to disembark in Calais. Holmes had been his usual taciturn self during the journey, breaking the silence only occasionally to use me as a sounding board for the theories he continued to develop about the Merchant.

We had caught a late afternoon ferry and then boarded a sleeper from Calais to Paris. As you can imagine, Holmes slept very little, preferring instead to indulge in several pipes and what I considered an unhealthy number of cigarettes.

I managed to doze for a few hours but was roused shortly after daybreak when all of a sudden, Holmes interrupted my reverie, remarking, "I do hope we are not making a mistake."

"What on Earth do you mean?"

"It is now obvious to me the Merchant wants us to come to Paris. I just hope he is not planning to strike somewhere in London during our absence."

"Do you think he is that clever?"

"Think? No, Watson, I am certain he is that cunning. If crime were a chess game, he would be a player of the highest caliber, perhaps a self-styled grandmaster such as the late William Lewis. Consider how many moves ahead he is able to plan. I just hope that our being summoned is more a show of braggadocio celebrating a victory of sorts than a clever gambit in our ongoing game that I have failed to anticipate."

"Holmes, you have bested him once already, and I am certain that you will do so again. At any rate, it is too late to lament about that possibility now," I remarked, glancing at my watch. "I believe that we shall arrive in Paris in less than an hour."

I could see the possibility that he might have been outmaneuvered by our foe had set my friend on edge. Once again he resorted to his pipe, and despite the hour, he soon had our compartment so filled with smoke that I had to step outside to admire the last vestiges of the French countryside before we arrived at our destination.

When the porter called out Paris, I once again entered our compartment and found my friend in much the same state as I had left him.

"I had thought to cable Lestrade as soon as we arrived in the Gare du Nord, but then I realized I have nothing to tell him. All we can do is hope for the best."

After we had disembarked, we hired a cab to take us to the Louvre, which is located in the very heart of the city in the first arrondissement. It was a fairly short drive, and as we stepped down, it was a clear day so I could easily discern the outline of the Eiffel Tower in the distance.

"This really is a magnificent metropolis," I remarked.

"They may call it the City of Lights, but it really is a city of monuments to mankind's insatiable thirst," observed Holmes waxing philosophic.

I was just about to compliment him on it, when he added, "It is also home to some of the most hardened criminals and cutthroats it has ever been my misfortune to encounter."

So much for philosophy, I thought.

After a walk across the expansive Coeur Napoleon, we entered the Louvre, and went immediately to a security guard, who fortunately for us spoke English, albeit with a pronounced Parisian accent.

"My name is Sherlock Holmes," my friend said, "and I should like very much to see your director. I do not have an appointment, but please tell him it is a matter of grave importance."

"Monsieur Homolle has been expecting you, Mr. Holmes," replied the guard. "Please follow me."

"The Director of the Louvre has been anticipating my visit, I wonder why," mused Holmes aloud as we walked.

Turning to us as he walked, the guard said, "Your associates informed us you would be along presently. Although he said, it might be a few weeks before you arrived as you were quite busy."

"My associates?" asked Holmes innocently.

"Oui, Messieurs Dearborn and Bates," replied the guard.

Holmes shot me a look that spoke volumes. We followed the guard downstairs. As we walked, he told us that the Louvre was in the early stages of planning to open an Islamic gallery sometime in the next few years, but at the moment, some of the pieces were being displayed as part of the Department of Decorative Arts while others were being readied for the new exhibit.

While I would have much preferred to enjoy a day taking in the many masterpieces that can be seen only in the Louvre, I knew Holmes was concerned not just with what had happened in the museum but with what might be taking place in London as well.

The guard led us into a storeroom, where a thin, ascetic-looking man was jotting down notes as he examined an ornate gold vase.

Turning to us, the man removed his spectacles and said, "Monsieur Holmes, I am Theophile Homolle, director of the Louvre, and I must say that is it a pleasure finally to meet you. Monsieur Dearborn informed us you would be arriving.

"And this, I assume, is your companion, Dr. Watson?"

"You assume correctly, Monsieur Homolle, and the pleasure is mine as well. However, I am afraid that I may have some disconcerting news for you? Would you prefer to discuss the situation here or in your office?"

"Since you are the bearer of such tidings, I will leave that decision to you, Monsieur Holmes."

After closing the door and making certain that we were alone, Holmes said "The men you know as Henry Dearborn and Edward Bates are not associates of mine. In fact, we believe that Mister Dearborn is an accomplished thief who may have made off with one or more of the Louvre's treasures."

"You cannot be serious, monsieur."

"The one you know as Bates is dead. His body was pulled from the Seine a few days ago. He had been stabbed to death."

"*Mon Dieu!*" exclaimed Homolle.

Holmes then proceeded to recount the tale of our various encounters with the Merchant. When he had finished, I could see Homolle was more than a little taken aback.

"When the men arrived at the Louvre, how did they present themselves?" asked Holmes.

"They told me in great detail about the attempted theft of the Tara Brooch and how they had assisted you in foiling the thief's plans. They then said that you anticipated a similar theft here, possibly involving the Baptistère de St. Louis. As you know, that is one of our most valuable treasures, and they explained the extra precautions that we might take to guard against the possibility of it being stolen."

"What exactly did they advise you?" asked Holmes.

"They inquired whether I had a safe in my office, and I informed them I did. Then they asked if it were large enough to contain the Baptisère. When I told them it was, they suggested storing it there and posting a guard outside the office around the clock. In fact, Mr. Bates carried the box containing the Baptistère to my office while Mr. Dearborn kept watch over the treasures here during our absence."

"Are you certain that the real Baptistère is in your safe?" I asked.

"*Absolutement*," Homolle replied emphatically.

"How can you be so sure?" I asked.

"The artist, who crafted the basin, for such it is really, was Muhammad Ibn al-Zain. It was probably originally designed for ceremonial hand-washings at banquets, and later, after it had made its way to France, it was used as a baptismal bowl. It is quite an incredible piece, adorned with court scenes and hunts."

Homolle might have gone on indefinitely, had not Holmes gently interrupted him. "You said you are certain the one in your office couldn't be a forgery. How can you be so sure?"

"The artisan, al-Zain, signed the bowl in several places. You cannot see them unless you look under the outer rim; there al-Zain has signed his name no fewer than six times."

"And that is the bowl in your safe?"

"Of that I am certain," replied Homolle.

"Did they show a particular interest in any of the other items?" Holmes inquired.

"Not that I can recall," Homolle replied.

Looking about and seeing a number of crates, Holmes asked, "And have you unpacked and examined everything?"

"All of the items have been unpacked and undergone an initial inspection. A number of artifacts have been repacked to prevent accidents. I am re-examining each individually now and taking notes which will become part of the exhibit. Once I have examined them a second time, they are locked in a separate storeroom."

"Were Bates and Dearborn aware of this other room?"

"They were, but they showed no particular interest in it," replied Homolle, anticipating Holmes' next question."

"Is there anything of great value in the items you have yet to examine for a second time?" asked Holmes.

Gazing at Holmes with what I can only describe as a look of utter disbelief on his face, Homolle replied sternly, "Monsieur Holmes, these are all incredibly rare artifacts. Each one of them is priceless."

"But if one were a collector of antiquities, say. What are the items in the Islamic collection that might arouse the passion of the true connoisseur?"

Pausing to consider, Homolle then replied, "There are several that fit that description, including 'The Eleanor of Aquitane Vase.' As its name indicates, the vase belonged to Eleanor of Aquitane, who, having inherited it from her grandfather, William IX, presented it to her first husband, King

Louis VII, as a wedding gift. The vase features a honeycomb pattern and as far as we know, it is the only piece of crystal in existence from that period carved in that pattern.

"During the medieval period, rock crystal was regarded as fossilized ice, so when you consider the craftsmanship and combine the glass vase with a mounting piece that features a circular base of silver and gold on which has been carved a semi-abstract floral design encrusted with jewels, the result is truly one of a kind. It is also the only known artifact that belonged to Eleanor."

"Excellent," replied Holmes. "May I ask how big the vase is?"

"It is approximately 15 inches tall by six inches wide."

"So, like the basin, it would be difficult to conceal under a coat if one wanted to smuggle it out of the Louvre."

"I should say that would be impossible," replied Homolle officiously. "We do have trained security guards here, Monsieur Holmes.

"Furthermore, Mr. Dearborn suggested the vase be stored in my safe as well."

"Interesting," said Holmes. "When you placed the vase in your safe, did Mr. Bates accompany you?"

"He did," replied Homolle.

"And Mr. Dearborn remained here?"

"Oui."

"And did you store the vase and the Baptistère in your safe on the same day?"

"No, Monsieur Holmes."

I thought that I could begin to see the traces of recognition dawning on Homolle's expression.

"So then, on at least two occasions, one of the most notorious thieves in Europe was left to his own devices in a room filled with priceless treasures."

I detected a note of panic in Homolle's voice when he replied, "But I was under the impression they were working with you."

"I am not casting aspersions," said Holmes. "I am merely trying to ascertain the order of events as completely as possible. Do you remember the days on which the vase and the Baptistère were brought to your office?"

"Indeed, the Baptistère was locked in the safe on a Tuesday around noon, and the vase was placed in the safe that following Thursday afternoon, shortly before the men left."

"Now, Mr. Homolle, just one more question. Are there any smaller items yet to be catalogued that you believe a thief might find irresistible?"

At that moment I saw the emotions of recognition and horror fighting for control of the man's face. Monsieur Theophile Homolle was quite obviously a man in turmoil.

Chapter 11

In an anguished cry, Homolle wailed, "The Pyxis of al-Mughira!"

With that he rushed to a crate, pried off the top with a crowbar and began pulling various smaller boxes from within. Finally, he turned to us holding a box perhaps a foot square whose top had been secured with a hasp and a small padlock. The relief on his face was evident as he said, "It is still here."

"What is a pyxis?" I asked confused.

Holmes replied, "Generally speaking, a pyxis is a cylindrical box used for storing jewels, aromatic substances or cosmetics. Unless I am mistaken, the pyxis to which Monsieur Homolle is referring is an elaborately carved ivory cylinder made from a single elephant tusk that was a gift to the then-eighteen-year-old Prince al-Mughira, the son of the deceased caliph Abd al-Raḥmān III."

"Exactly, Monsieur Holmes," said Homolle as he was searching a large ring of keys which he had fished from his pocket for the one to open the lock. "It is among the best surviving examples of the royal ivory-carving tradition in Al-Andalus, which you might call Islamic Spain. We believe it was crafted in the late 10th century in the Madinat al-Zahra workshops, and its intricate and exceptional carving sets it apart from many other examples. Moreover, it features an inscription and figurative work which are important for understanding the traditions of ivory carving and Islamic art in Al-Andalus."

Finally finding the key, he opened the box and extracted a purple velvet sack that had been secured with heavy twine. Loosening the knot, he reached in and his face turned ashen.

"We have been robbed," he screamed. Instead of an ivory cylinder, he withdrew his hand holding a round wooden box that looked to be some six inches tall and perhaps five inches across. He was just about to hurl the box across the room when Holmes intervened.

"Monsieur Homolle, please do not do that. The box may contain valuable clues that will help us recover the pyxis."

Almost grudgingly, he handed the box to Holmes, who began to examine it. Opening the lid, he looked inside. "Hello, what's this?" Pulling a small envelope from within, he looked at it and a wry smile crossed his face.

"What is it, Monsieur Holmes? Is it a ransom demand? We will pay anything to recover the pyxis!" Homolle stated.

"I do not believe it is a ransom demand," replied my friend. "As it is addressed to me, shall I open it?"

"By all means," replied Homolle.

Pulling a penknife from his pocket, Holmes carefully slit the flap and extracted a sheet of ivory-colored notepaper. Unfolding it, he read aloud:

"The early bird does indeed catch the worm.

Turnabout is fair play, Mr. Holmes."

"Monsieur Holmes, what does it mean?"

"It means that I am determined to recover the pyxis for you," said my friend, "but I am going to need your help."

"Anything, Monsieur Holmes. Anything at all."

"To begin with, say nothing of the theft to anyone. Not to your fellow museum officials, not to the Surete; speak of this to no one."

"And you are certain you can recover it?"

"If Holmes says that he will recover it, then you must trust him," I interjected. "He has bested the greatest criminal minds in all of Europe."

"It will not be quick nor will it be easy, and your patience may be tested, but I promise you that the Pyxis of al-Mughira will be returned to the Louvre."

The quiet confidence with which Holmes uttered his pronouncement seemed to reassure Homolle somewhat. "Is there anything you need? Anything I can do for you?" asked Homolle.

"If you have no objections, I should like to take this wooden box and the bag and crate that contained it as well as the lock with me."

"Please, they are yours."

"I am afraid that we must return to London at once," said Holmes. "I fear that our trip here may have been little more than a diversion in order to allow the thief free rein there in my absence."

"I will escort you out, messieurs. The security guard would never let you leave with that box in any event."

A few minutes later, we were walking back across the Coeur Napoleon. Turning to me, Holmes said, "My respect for this rascal continues to grow. He challenges me directly, Watson, and then he has the effrontery to tweak me."

"Holmes, there was no way, you could have foreseen this."

"That is quite true; nevertheless, here we are. He knew enough to anticipate me, and he calculated my every move in advance."

"Just as you anticipated his every move with the Tara Brooch."

"True. I believe I can find some small measure of solace in that victory, but this next round is one that we *must* win."

"Do you think the box or the crate will provide you with any clues?"

"Not really," replied my friend. "Our adversary is far too clever for that."

"Then why take it?"

"I have my reasons," he replied enigmatically.

Our return to London was quite similar to our journey to Paris. Holmes said little and smoked a great deal. With his lens, he pored over the box, the lock, the bag and the note, seemingly committing the details of each to memory.

When we were once again in our rooms at Baker Street, he sent out about six telegrams and dispatched a messenger to ask Lestrade to drop by when the opportunity permitted. '

The next morning, I awoke to find Holmes perusing the papers. After he had finished, I looked at him and asked: "What's to be done?"

"Lestrade will be here shortly and rather than repeat myself, I would beg your indulgence until he arrives."

About thirty minutes later, I heard the bell. Holmes glanced at his watch and said, "If nothing else, the good inspector is prompt."

When Lestrade entered the room, Holmes rose, greeted him and asked if he would prefer coffee or tea.

"Whatever you have on hand is fine," said Lestrade. "Don't trouble Mrs. Hudson."

After Holmes had poured coffee for Lestrade and refilled our cups, he said, "Inspector, what I am about to tell you must not leave this room." He then told Lestrade everything that had happened at the Louvre, omitting only the note from the Merchant.

When he had finished, Lestrade looked at him and said, "How are we going to catch this bloke? Obviously, he poses a threat to museums and collection owners everywhere. How can we possibly know where he is going to strike next?"

"We cannot, and that is why I am going to need your assistance."

"What would you like me to do, Mr. Holmes?"

"If you could, cable your counterparts, both on the Continent as well as in America and Canada, and ask them to inform you of the theft of any unusual *objets d'art.* I think that will offer us a starting place. We know what attracts our Merchant, to use Watson's sobriquet for him. He is interested in one-of-a-kind objects that are sought after by wealthy collectors. Whether he contacts them or they him, remains to be seen.

"Just ask them to make you aware if such an item, and it can be anything from a rare book to a gem to a painting, should suddenly go missing."

"How many countries would you like me to contact?" asked Lestrade.

"Cast your net as far and as wide as you can, this is no ordinary thief we are endeavoring to capture."

"I shall start today, Mr. Holmes."

After Lestrade had departed, I said to Holmes, "And what are we to do?"

He looked at me and said, "Once again, there is really nothing we can do but wait. We have returned to the beginning as it were."

"You cannot be serious," I exclaimed.

"Ah, Watson. I think the trip to Paris taught me one thing."

"Oh?"

"It is imperative that somehow I find a way seize the initiative. I must devise a plan that involves something he simply cannot resist. I just told Lestrade to cast a wide net. To return to that fishing metaphor, which I employed earlier, we must be the patient anglers. We must select just the right bait, seek out the proper location, cast our lines carefully and then wait patiently. Just as we cannot make the fish bite, so we cannot make the thief steal. However, if we are able to put everything in order, we can land this thief as surely as the proper fly will appeal to that salmon swimming upstream in the River Tyne."

"You make it sound so easy," I said.'

"It will be anything but. We will have to take some people into our confidence, something I am always loath to do. Then we will have to fashion a credible scenario with a prize that our Merchant deems irresistible. It will take time and planning, but, in the end, I promise you, we will settle our accounts with this Merchant."

I was tempted to ask Holmes why he had neglected to tell Lestrade about the note at the Louvre, but seeing him in such a determined mood, I decided to broach it at a later date – if at all.

Chapter 12

Left with no other recourse, we continued to "stand and wait," as Milton says in his Sonnet 19. One day passed slowly into the next; occasionally, Lestrade would drop by and brief Holmes on various thefts or attempted thefts committed in foreign lands. I remember there were two that seemed to pique my friend's interest.

The first involved a letter signed by Abraham Lincoln that had gone missing from the National Archives in Washington, D.C. "It is just a single page," explained Lestrade. "In fact, it is a telegram President Lincoln dispatched to one of his officers in St. Louis, inquiring about the release of a certain Dr. Bassett. What makes it valuable is the signature."

"When was it stolen?" asked Holmes.

"Truth be told, it may not have been stolen," replied Lestrade, "but it is most definitely missing. As to when it was nicked, if it was, they really can't say for certain."

"It may have been our man, but I am inclined to doubt it," replied Holmes. "At any rate, there's precious little to go on since they are not even certain when or even if it has actually been stolen."

"I agree Mr. Holmes, but I thought you would like to know about it."

"Thank you, Lestrade. Should anything else develop, please keep me informed."

"I will do that," said the inspector, who then took his leave.

As one who abhorred idleness, Holmes busied himself with a number of diverse cases, including one I have titled "The Missing Manuscript," which saw my friend uncover a long-lost copy of Lord Byron's memoirs. In 1824, the only copy of what is believed to be a fairly salacious tale of the Romantic poet's life had been burned by his then-publisher, John Murray, and several of the poet's closest friends. They feared the memoirs were entirely too risqué for the public. Holmes later confided in me that they had also been apprehensive their closeness with Byron might sully their own reputations should the memoirs ever be published.

However, the heirs of the publisher never gave up hope that a second copy might exist, and eventually they enlisted Holmes in their quest to locate it.

With very little effort, my friend discovered where the *enfant terrible* of Georgian England had concealed his own copy of his reminiscences. He then turned it over to the publisher's heirs, and, sadly, its fate remains unknown to this day.

When I asked Holmes about the contents, he echoed the sentiments of William Gifford, an advisor to Byron's publisher in 1824, who had opined that the book was "fit only for a brothel." However, Holmes added that in his view, the memoirs were a rollicking good tale that might have turned proper Victorian society on its head.

As you might expect, Holmes cared little about the disposition of Byron's apparently sordid tale, and when pressed he would only say, "The case is solved, the client is satisfied, what more can I ask?"

Several weeks passed during which Holmes kept himself busy updating one of his previously published monographs and rendering aid to a variety of individuals who sought his help. Finally, perhaps a month after his last visit, Lestrade stopped by one afternoon.

"I believe you may find this of interest, Mr. Holmes," he announced.

"Do tell, Lestrade."

"Apparently, there was an attempted theft at the Anichkov Palace in St. Petersburg."

The change in Holmes' demeanor was immediate. He was suddenly all attention. "Do you have any details, Lestrade?"

"Precious few, unfortunately. Apparently, one of the servants was found trussed up and unconscious in a pantry. The deception was soon discovered, and the would-be thief fled the moment the alarm was sounded."

"Excellent, Lestrade. You described it as an 'attempted theft.' May I assume nothing was taken?"

"As far as the authorities were able to ascertain, the thief was forced to flee empty-handed."

"Well, that certainly sounds as though it might have been our man. After all, it takes planning and more than a bit of nerve to attempt to rob a royal palace."

"I wonder what he might have been after," I mused.

"I suppose we will never know," Lestrade replied.

"Yes, more's the pity. Knowing the object of his attention might have allowed us to marshal our forces around any similar objects that might be have made their way to the kingdom. You said it was the Anichkov Palace?"

"I did," reiterated Lestrade.

"What type of treasure could he have hoped to find there?" I added.

"I do get ahead of myself," Holmes replied. "Lestrade, this is an avenue that bears pursuing. Please let me know if you should receive any further word from your friends in Russia. And by the way, Inspector, when I said cast your net far and wide, I had no idea you would take me so seriously. Well done!"

I thought Lestrade was as close to blushing as I had ever seen him, but instead he replied. "Thank you, Mr. Holmes. And should I hear anything further, you will be the first to know."

As he turned to leave, he added, "And if you should hear anything about the theater thefts in the East End, you will do the same?"

After Lestrade had departed, Holmes looked at me and said, "I see you are meeting with your literary agent today."

"How could you know that? We arranged the meeting just yesterday, and I haven't spoken of it to anyone."

"It's Friday, Watson. Of late, you have taken to indulging your aversion to shaving on Fridays, unless you have an important appointment. Yet here you are clean-shaven and wearing a tie, which tells me that it is a meeting of some import, and the satchel, in which you carry your manuscripts is sitting ready by your chair."

"You don't miss much, do you?" I observed.

"I see and I observe," he replied placidly.

"And what will you do this afternoon?" I asked.

"I have some correspondence to take care of, and then I may visit my brother at the Diogenes Club."

Although he said it rather innocently, I suspected he would be consulting with Mycroft about the Merchant of Menace and possibly the attempted theft in Russia. Knowing better than to press him on the matter, I refrained, fully aware that Holmes would eventually reveal what had transpired.

My meeting with my agent went quite well, and I enjoyed a lunch of stuffed salmon with a very dry pinot gris. Contented, I returned to our rooms to find Holmes in his blue dressing gown, curled up in his chair, leafing through one of his many indices.

"I did not expect you back this early," I remarked.

"Nor I you, but Mycroft had a great many things to which he must attend, so our meeting was quite brief. Unfortunately, I will not know whether it has been productive for several days."

"Oh?"

"I have asked Mycroft to make a number of inquiries for me. I rather think his agents will be somewhat more discrete – and effective – in their efforts than Lestrade's counterparts. They will also be more thorough. Lestrade is primarily looking at museums and art galleries, but there are many other places where valuables may reside – even if only on a temporary basis."

Holmes' words would prove to be prophetic, and although his preoccupation with the Merchant appeared to have faded into the background, it was merely a façade that covered his intense involvement in bringing to justice a foe who had so far eluded him and, in one instance, had actually bested him.

Periodically, he would receive a wire, presumably directed to him by one of Mycroft's agents, and on a few of those occasions, I thought I detected a rare look of satisfaction on his face.

Once, I summoned up the nerve to ask him, "Good news?"

He responded by saying, "Come now, Watson, don't be coy. What you are really asking is: What have I heard and have I made any progress? Let me put it this way: Slowly but surely, my plan is coming together. I am constructing my web and quite an intricate one it is; however, I must do so in such a manner that not only are the strings invisible and the enticement irresistible, but so that there is absolutely no possibility of escape.

"Believe me, old friend, there is much that I should like to share with you, and I will certainly do so at a more propitious time."

And so like Holmes, I found myself suffering in silence as our seemingly endless vigil continued. However, I am the first to admit that he is far more adroit at bearing that burden than I.

The holidays came and went and we welcomed in the New Year of 1902 with little fanfare. Although other cases kept him busy, I could see, having known him for so long, that his every free moment was preoccupied with something, or perhaps I should more accurately say someone else entirely.

And so it was that one morning as we were enjoying our breakfast, I remarked, "The Guardian has a story about the Duchess of Marlborough returning from Russia. Apparently, she made quite the impression on Czar Nicholas and Czarina Alexandra, although why anyone would choose to winter in St. Petersburg baffles me."

"And you thought I would be interested in this?" inquired my friend archly.

"I was just making conversation. I find the fact that she is an American and yet moves effortlessly with kings and queens rather fascinating. I am also sure that it says something about our increased enlightenment when a 'commoner' can accomplish all that she has."

"Watson, you astound me! Commoner, indeed! The woman is the daughter of William Vanderbilt, the American railroad tycoon, and her marriage to Charles Spencer-Churchill, the Duke of Marlborough and Earl of Sunderland, while it may have been advantageous to both parties, was due more to the Machiavellian machinations of her mother than any efforts on the part of the blind bow boy."

"Why Holmes you sound as though you know the woman."

"Truth be told, I have met her on a two different occasions although I rather doubt she would remember me. By the way, is there any mention of jewelry in that article?"

"Not that I saw, why do you ask?"

"I am told that in addition to meeting the Czar and Czarina, the Duchess also had an audience with the Czar's mother, Maria Feodorovna, the Dowager Empress, who, I am told, loves nothing more than to dazzle foreign visitors with her extensive collection of jeweled baubles and other treasures."

"Holmes, you never fail to amaze me! How could you possibly know of the Dowager Empress' penchant for jewelry?"

"Do you not recall the Exposition Universelle in Paris two years ago?"

"Of course, what of it?"

"One of the judges of the jewelry was a certain Karl Gustavovich Fabergé, who is now more commonly known as Peter Carl Fabergé. Although he was not allowed to compete, owing to his status as a judge, he was allowed to exhibit."

"And what was it that he exhibited?"

"Fabergé is a master craftsman, who, for the last 17 years has been creating Imperial Easter Eggs for the Czars of Russia to present to their wives on their holiest of holy days. I believe the custom originated in 1885 when Czar Alexander III commissioned an egg for his wife, Maria Feodorovna. Fabergé's first effort is known as the 'Hen Egg.' When opened, the opaque shell of white enamel revealed a matte yellow-gold yolk. When, in turn, that was opened, a multicolored gold hen could be found inside. The hen, which believe it or not, also opens, contained a miniature diamond replica of the imperial crown from which a small ruby pendant was suspended. I have it on the best authority that it is breathtaking, but that it pales in comparison to his later creations."

"You can't be serious! You mean to say in a country as troubled as Russia, the czar spends a fortune each year on a bauble?"

"I am quite serious. In fact, it has only worsened, for Czar Nicholas now has two eggs created each year – one for his wife and one for his mother."

"It is positively unseemly," I exclaimed.

"You do realize that Queen Victoria possessed any number of pieces created by Fabergé, including a diamond-studded notebook the Czar and Czarina, who happened to be Victoria's granddaughter, gave her for Christmas in 1896. Given their relationships, the British, Russian and Danish royal families all have fairly extensive collections of Fabergé's creations."

"Yes, but there is a world of difference between the life of a peasant in Russia and a working man here in Britain," I said.

"Is there really?" Holmes inquired. "I wonder how the residents of some of our poorer sections might feel about that remark.

"Be that as it may, Fabergé continues to outdo himself each year. In fact, his creation for 1900 was an egg paying homage to Russia's greatest engineering achievement, the Trans-Siberian Railway. I am told the egg itself rests on three golden griffins and is topped by a Romanov eagle. On a broad silver band around the middle is an engraved map that traces the railway's 4,000-mile route from St. Petersburg to Vladivostok, with each station marked by a precious stone.

"Inside the egg is a miniature train that when assembled is a foot long. You wind it with a golden key and it actually runs. The engine is made of platinum with diamond headlights and each of the five coaches has been crafted from gold."

"My word! But what has this French jeweler to do with the Merchant?"

"Actually, he's not French at all. Although he is of Huguenot descent, he was born in St. Petersburg, and as you might expect, his father was also a jeweler. As for the Merchant, few people outside of Russia know this, but Fabergé has created eggs for one or two other people besides the Czar. Starting in 1898, he began making eggs for Alexander Ferdinandovich Kelch, a Siberian gold mine industrialist, who gave them as gifts to his wife. As you might expect the Kelch eggs are not nearly as elaborate as the Imperial Eggs, and most are merely copies of Fabergé's earlier efforts."

"But the Merchant?" I insisted.

"I have it on the most reliable authority that Fabergé recently completed an egg for a non-Russian; it is said to be the first of its kind."

"You don't mean the Duchess of Marlborough?"

"Indeed, I do. Her Ladyship is now the proud owner of a Fabergé egg, affectionately known as the Pink Serpent Egg. The egg, which was inspired by a Louis XVI clock, features a silver snake coiling up from a triangular base. On a band around the middle of the egg are the hours in Roman numerals. So while the snake's head remains stationary, one can estimate the time by examining the band, which is actually a revolving dial. I'm told it's similar to the Imperial Blue Serpent Egg, created in 1895."

"So you have been planning this all along?"

"Let us say I have been cautiously optimistic. Things really started looking up when I learned that Fabergé had accepted the commission from the Duchess. You never know how people are going to react to recently titled Americans. I must admit I was fearful my plans had come to naught when Lestrade informed us of the attempted theft at the Anichkov Palace. I don't think I have ever been so relieved to learn that a thief escaped."

"You cannot be serious," I said.

"I am most serious," replied Holmes. "Call it vanity, if you will, but I should like to be the one who finally brings this Merchant to justice, if I am able."

That last remark told me how personal this case had become for my friend. For him to react as he did was, I thought, quite telling.

"So am I to assume that the Duchess' egg is to serve your 'bait'?"

"I think the Pink Serpent Egg will be impossible to resist. I believe someone saw Fabergé's eggs at the Exposition. Whether the jeweler refused to accept the commission or the price was too dear, we shall never know. It follows then that our buyer and the Merchant crossed paths and arrived at some sort of agreement. That would explain the attempted theft in Russia. Given that failure, his options for obtaining a Fabergé egg are quite limited. So as you say, we have the bait. Now we must set about casting our line."

"How do you know the Merchant won't strike before you are ready?"

"Watson, do you think I would go to all this trouble and then allow my bait to sit unattended. No, my friend, I am leaving nothing to chance. With Mycroft's help, I have made certain the egg is in a safe place and shall remain there until it is time to spring our trap."

"I suspected Mycroft played a role in this."

"My brother has proved an invaluable resource thus far. He still has one or two tasks to carry out, but I have faith in his persuasive abilities."

"Why is he helping you?"

"I merely suggested the possibility that if the Merchant could rob the Louvre successfully and nearly get away with a similar treasure from the British Museum, how safe were any of our national treasures – including the Crown Jewels."

"And may I assume that one of Mycroft's tasks is to persuade the Duchess to allow you to use her egg as your bait?"

"That has already been taken care of. Mycroft has had the government purchase the egg for the Duke and Duchess, so she really has nothing to lose. Once the Merchant has been captured, with their cooperation, the egg is theirs free and clear."

"Holmes, that really is quite an achievement!"

"Save your praise, Watson. Thus far all we have are the rudiments of a plan. As you well know, the devil is in the details, and there is no shortage of those that must be addressed before we can even consider our next step forward."

"I have faith in you my friend."

Holmes then looked at me and in a rare moment of absolute candor, he replied. "Thank you, old friend. I can only hope that your faith has not been misplaced."

Chapter 13

Over the next several weeks, Holmes was constantly busy at a variety of different tasks, and his moods seemed quite wild and unpredictable. Some nights I would return home to find him chipper and talkative while other nights he would allow himself to slip into the depths of despair. On those occasions when his mood was lighter, we would converse about an array of subjects from art to opera to theater, while on those darker nights, he would seek the solace of his pipe and shag.

One night, Holmes and I were invited to attend a run-through performance of *The Emerald Isle*, which is subtitled *The Caves of Carrig-Cleena*. It had opened the previous year and run more than 200 performances at the Savoy. Now it was headed for a revival in New York, at the famed Herald Square Theatre.

I have always loved the Savoy, and the fact that it was the first theatre to use electric lighting had made quite an impression on me – far more than the play, which was a bit of stuff and nonsense about an English professor of elocution attempting to re-educate the Irish. As we left the theatre and were riding in a cab back to Baker Street, we were forced to detour because of a fire and so we found ourselves passing the Egyptian Hall in Piccadilly.

Noting the marquee, I asked Holmes, "Have you ever seen Maskelyne and Cooke perform?"

"Are you talking about the magicians?" he asked.

"Yes, I am told they put on quite a show, In fact, they say Maskelyne can even make people float in the air!"

"So I have heard," replied Holmes. "I believe the term he employs is 'levitation.'"

"That is it, exactly," I said. "I believe that at some performances he even makes the woman he is levitating disappear."

"That is why they are sometimes call 'illusionists,' Watson. What you think you are seeing and what you are actually seeing may, in fact, be two quite different things.

"However, I will give Maskelyne his due. I have heard that he has made thousands of pennies disappear all over London."

"You don't say," I exclaimed.

"I do, indeed," replied Holmes. "After all, when he wasn't making people float about and vanish, he found time to invent the pay toilet. Now that is a trick indeed, to get people to pay for taking care of their bodily functions."

I laughed in spite of myself, and the conversation quickly turned to other topics. I could see that Holmes was enjoying his respite from dealing with the Merchant and having to labor over his plans to thwart the thief's next attempt. In fact, the evening was so pleasant that when we arrived at Baker Street, we both enjoyed a second nightcap before turning in.

The next morning, I awoke around nine and was not surprised to learn that Holmes had eaten and left our rooms sometime earlier. With nothing to do, I set about transcribing the notes from one of our recent cases. I had nearly completed my task, when Holmes returned, and said, "I do hope Mrs. Hudson has lunch ready. I am quite hungry today."

Since food seldom mattered to Holmes, I took that as a positive sign and inquired, "You have received some good news then?"

"Indeed, I have," he replied. "I now know with some specificity the nature of the trap I plan to set, but there are still mountains of details that need be addressed."

"Then where have you been all morning then?"

"In due time, Watson. I have no desire to spoil any of my surprises."

"After all these years, you still don't trust me to keep a secret. I must say, Holmes, I am just a bit nettled, and I believe justifiably so."

"Don't be cross, old boy. Believe me when I tell you many things are still in the most rudimentary planning stages. When I have something of substance to share, I certainly will."

Mollified by his comments, I was able to enjoy the lunch that Mrs. Hudson had just brought into the room.

That afternoon, Holmes received a telegraph from his brother, requesting that he meet him at the Diogenes Club that evening at 8.

"I know this is the night when you often play billiards with Thurston, but I was wondering if you might care to accompany me."

"I would be delighted," I replied. "Let Thurston take someone else's money for a change."

After dinner, we both enjoyed a cigarette and then Holmes looked at his watch. "It's such a pleasant evening out, if we leave now, we can walk to Pall Mall. Are you game?"

I said that I was, and so we set out, estimating that we should arrive at The Diogenes at just about the appointed hour. The evening was unseasonably warm, and as we strolled through St. James Square, I was pleased to note the first signs of spring. Although there were no flowers, I could discern an abundance of green shoots, jutting up from the earth. It was then I realized Easter would be upon us in just a few days, and I wondered if the timing of this meeting had anything to do with the Imperial Easter Eggs.

When we arrived at the Diogenes Club, we were shown into the Stranger's Room, the only room in the club where talking is permitted. A few minutes later, Mycroft joined us. After he had settled his considerable girth into a wing chair that seemed to groan under the weight, he asked, "Would you care for some refreshments? Coffee, perhaps? Or a brandy?"

"You didn't summon me here for the refreshments," Holmes responded.

"No, that's quite true," said Mycroft. "I thought I might enjoy a brief respite from having to deal with the planned ascension of Alfonso XIII to the throne of Spain. However, as you seem determined to get to the point as quickly as possible, I shall oblige you. I have spoken with the Duke and Duchess of Marlborough. She would be willing to help us even were she not being compensated. I don't know that the same can be said of His Lordship."

"Yes, I'd rather heard that financial considerations were of the utmost importance to him."

"Indeed. At any rate, with some slight encouragement, he has agreed to allow us the use of any site we may wish in order to apprehend this Merchant of yours."

"I thought that we were limited to Blenheim Palace."

"Initially, we were," replied Mycroft. "However, I want this rascal captured as quickly as you do, so with a little leverage, I managed to convince the powers that be to allow us the use of Marlborough House if it should suit you."

Holmes paused for a moment as he weighed his options. Turning to Mycroft, he said, "While that is certainly an attractive offer, I still believe that Blenheim would better suit our needs. It has a few obvious advantages over any of the Duke's other holdings, including Marlborough House."

"I rather thought you might say that," replied Mycroft. "Now, if you will just let me know when you are ready, I will inform the Duchess. She is simply dying to show off her Fabergé egg. She believes it is the only one that Fabergé has executed for a non-Russian."

"Isn't it?" replied Holmes. "For if the situation has changed, that could certainly force us to alter our plans."

"As far as we know it is," replied Mycroft. "However, one of my agents in Russia has heard rumors to the effect that the jeweler might also be crafting an egg for Beatrice Rothschild. At any rate, as of now, the Duchess possesses the only Fabergé egg outside of Russia, but that may not be the case for very much longer. Truth be told, she is so pleasant that I have not the heart to tell her about the possibility."

"You? Sentimental?" scoffed Holmes. "At any rate, this does rather add a little extra pressure to pull things together quickly as time has now become a factor."

"How so?" I asked.

"I think what Sherlock is trying to say," Mycroft replied, "is that to some degree we are ready for the Merchant. We have at least the outline of a plan in place to effect his capture should he try to steal the Duchess' Fabergé egg. The Rothschilds do not even know of this thief's existence nor do they have their egg yet. Were I this Merchant, I should certainly choose the path of least resistance, and that is why we must move at a quickened pace, while it appears there is but a single path to be taken."

Rising, Holmes said to Mycroft, "You have hit it exactly. Now, I must take my leave, I have plans to finalize and other business to which I must attend. I leave the Empire in your capable hands, dear brother. Thank you for your help and your offer of hospitality. I shall let you know as soon as everything is in place."

With that we departed the Diogenes Club. As the sky was now threatening and we could hear thunder in the distance, we decided to take a cab back to our rooms.

During the ride, Holmes said, "The possibility of another egg outside of Russia could prove fatal to our plans. I must admit I had not even entertained that prospect. As a result, we must proceed with all due haste."

"If there is anything I can do to assist you, all you have to do is ask," I said.

"If you are serious, Watson …"

"You know I am, Holmes."

"Then, have you ever been to Blenheim Palace?"

"No," I laughed, "I seldom move in those rarified circles. However, I will admit I had always hoped to be invited. I have hears such wonderful things about the palace."

"Well then, consider yourself invited. I should like you to visit Blenheim as soon as possible. Get the lay of the land, so to speak, and then report back to me."

"Is this a day trip? Or am I am to spend the night?"

"Whichever you prefer. The key is to be on the lookout for places where we might trap the Merchant."

"Do you mean in the house or on the grounds or both?"

"As I told Lestrade some time ago, cast a wide net. If you see a spot you think might lend itself to an ambush of any kind, take notes and, if possible, add a sketch. I cannot emphasize how important this is, Watson. We must bring the Merchant to justice there, and we must not fail. We will be given only so many opportunities."

Initially, I must confess that I thought Holmes might be trying to send me on some sort of fool's errand, but I could tell by the tone in his voice and his demeanor he considered this a matter of some urgency.

"I will leave first thing in the morning," I promised.

"Excellent! I shall wire Mycroft and he will tell them to expect you." With that he dashed off a quick note as soon as we had arrived home and within minutes he had dispatched the buttons to the Diogenes Club.

"You don't think there will be any problems, do you?"

"I rather doubt it as Mycroft's name can open a great many doors in a great many places."

Early the next morning, I grabbed the bag I had packed the night before and, without bidding Holmes, who had not yet arisen, farewell, I descended the stairs and hailed a cab for Paddington Station.

It is some three hours by rail to Oxford, but between reading the paper I had purchased and enjoying the scenery, once we had left the environs of London, the time passed rather quickly. Holmes proved better than his word, for there was a carriage waiting for me at the station to take me to Blenheim.

The driver informed me his name was Raymond Imp, and he and his wife, Catherine, had been at Blenheim for more than 20 years. He told me to call him Ray and then said we had approximately an hour's journey ahead of us. "Have you ever been to Blenheim, Dr. Watson?" he asked. Looking at the man, who was shorter than I but much more powerfully built, I thought his surname belied his appearance. I also recall thinking this is one Imp I should like to have on my side in a donnybrook.

When I admitted that I had not, he began to recount the history of the estate. He was so full of facts and anecdotes, I told him he had missed his vocation and he should have pursued a career as a writer. Among the interesting tidbits he imparted was that Blenheim is the only country estate in England that is not a royal residence but is still called a palace.

He also outlined its history and how the palace, which was built in the first quarter of the 18th century, has 187 rooms, making it one of England's largest houses. According to Ray, the palace was named for the Battle of Blenheim, and was originally intended to be a reward to John Churchill, the first Duke of Marlborough, for his military triumphs against the French and Bavarians in the War of the Spanish Succession. He then touched upon the subject of political infighting that had led to Marlborough's exile, and his eventual return after the death of Queen Anne.

The estate comprises some 2,000 acres, and one must cross a bridge over the River Glyme to arrive via the front gate. With Ray's stories filling the time, the hour passed quickly and it was just before noon when we crested the small hill and descended toward the bridge over the Glyme. As we drew closer, I began to realize that to do this magnificent estate justice was far beyond my poor powers. Everywhere you looked, there was something to see. In the distance, I spied formal gardens that would probably be awash with multi-colored blooms in another month or two. There were two lakes which Ray had told me were man-made and many other sights upon which I simply cannot dwell on here.

As I ascended the steps, I was met by Childers, the head butler; and Mrs. Thorson, the head housekeeper. A servant took my bag and I was shown into the Great Hall. Standing on the marble floor, I felt like an intruder. Rows of busts ensconced in large niches on both sides of the second-floor level gazed down on me accusingly as though they knew I did not belong there. Above them was a clerestory that flooded the hall with natural light on sunny days. On the ceiling had been painted a magnificent oval mural that I later learned was an allegorical representation of the successes of first Duke of Marlborough, who was depicted as Mars while Queen Anne was represented as Britannia, mistress of the World, on which she was seated. To say it all was a trifle overwhelming is to yield to my better angel, and we will leave it at that.

Neither the Duke nor Duchess was at the estate, but I could see where a great deal of the money the Duke had received upon marrying Consuelo Vanderbilt had been lavished. Childers led me on a rather lengthy tour, which given the size of Blenheim was not surprising. The rooms were all sumptuously decorated and one room easily outdid the one before it.

I was also informed by Childers that the design and building of the palace between 1705 and 1722 was considered by many as the birth of a new style of architecture and its landscaped park, the brainchild of Lancelot "Capability" Brown, was generally regarded as a "naturalistic Versailles."

Although I did not enter the private quarters of either the Duke or Duchess, I was shown where they were, so that I might include the locations in my report.

I tried to imagine where the Duchess, and Holmes, might want to display the egg in order to capture the Merchant. After I had finished the tour, I decided I would suggest that the egg be exhibited in either the Main Salon or the Long Library, although I was leaning towards the former.

I reasoned that the three doors to the Main Hall could be easily guarded before and during the gala. Although for the life of me, I could not figure out how the Merchant thought he might escape with the egg. After all, the Duchess must have a safe of some sort for her jewels, and I was pretty certain that it could also provide a safe haven for Fabergé's creation when it wasn't being displayed.

I also reasoned if guards were posted on the bridge, they could prevent anyone from escaping that way, which meant that the only way out would be through the expansive park behind the estate.

I made a rough sketch of the estate for Holmes, focusing on the locations that might come into play in our adventure. However, even as I did I had my doubts about selecting this venue with its myriad rooms and sprawling grounds for what I hoped would be our final confrontation with the Merchant of Menace.

After all, I reasoned, Marlborough House could be more easily secured while attempting to cover all the possible entries and exits from Blenheim was certain to prove a daunting task.

When I looked at my watch, I was stunned to discover that it was nearly five o'clock. Although Childers offered me dinner and a room, and I was sorely tempted to accept his hospitality, I decided that for the moment I had seen everything I needed to see. Furthermore, I knew that I should be returning in the very near future, so after a light repast, I found myself back in the carriage with Ray at the reins. Although he was as talkative as ever, I suddenly found myself overcome by fatigue. Eventually, he lapsed into silence, and when we reached the station, he bid me a fond farewell. I assured him that we would be seeing each other quite soon and told him how invaluable his insights had proved.

When I arrived back at Baker Street, it was nearing midnight. I ascended the stairs quietly but need not have troubled myself, for when I entered the flat, I found a note from Holmes waiting for me on the table.

"Watson,

I have been called out of town for a day or two. I shall be in touch. In the meantime, see if you are able to determine the precise dimensions of the Duchess' Fabergé egg — both height and weight. Try to avoid contacting the Duchess or anyone on her staff.

Sincerely,

Holmes"

Chapter 14

I had no idea what to make of Holmes' missive, but I was determined to carry out my friend's instructions. Uncertain who else might know such details about the egg besides the Duchess, I decided, as per his instructions, I would turn to her only as the absolute last resort. In a bit of a quandary, I considered asking Dr. Smith at the London Museum. After all, I reasoned, in his capacity there he had to have handled all types of precious artifacts, many of which probably required insurance. And then it hit me, who would know more about such items than another jeweler?

Although it was overcast with a threatening sky, I decided to take my umbrella and walk to Asprey's & Co. on New Bond Street. After a stroll of some 20 minutes, I was greeted at the front door by George, the manager. I had known him for several years and had offered him some marital advice while Holmes and I were investigating the theft of the Stone of Destiny the previous year.

He greeted me effusively, saying, "Dr. Watson, it has been far too long." Looking about, he added, "Mr. Holmes, he is not with you?"

"No," I replied. "He is working on a case that has taken him away from London for a few days."

I don't know if I imagined it, but it seemed as though George were relieved Holmes was not present. He then asked, "How may I assist you, Dr. Watson?"

I told him the information, I was looking for, and he suggested we adjourn to his office. Once we had settled ourselves, he said, "It is curious you should bring up the Fabergé eggs at this time."

"Oh?" I asked.

"Come now, Dr. Watson. I have just learned about the Duchess of Marlborough returning with her egg, and now here you are asking questions about the same topic. It does not take the skill of Mr. Holmes to divine a connection of some sort."

"Your discretion would be greatly appreciated by all involved," I said.

"And you shall have it," he replied. "So tell me what it is exactly you would like to know."

"If possible, Mr. Holmes would like to learn the exact dimensions and the weight of the Duchess' egg."

"Then you have come to the right place," he said, beaming. Opening his desk drawer, George pulled out a folder. Placing several pages in front of me, he said, "Those are sketches of the Blue Serpent Egg, which served as a model for the egg the Duchess now possesses. As you can see, this creation supersedes mere jewelry. This is art."

Looking at the intricate workmanship depicted in the drawings, I was inclined to agree. George then handed me a new sheet with a sketch of the egg and the dimensions next to each section. All told, the egg stood seven-and-three-quarter inches high and was two-and-three quarter inches in diameter at its widest point. A note printed neatly at the bottom of the page said the egg weighed just slightly more than one-and-a-half pounds."

"This is exactly what Holmes was looking for! How on Earth did you come by it?"

"I had the great pleasure of meeting Mr. Fabergé and his head jeweler, Michael Perchin, at the Universelle Exposition in Paris last year. I broached the idea of possibly crafting a line of high-end reproductions. I believe that many people would like to own a Fabergé egg, and since most can't afford to purchase an original, we would be filling a demand.

"I had drawn up a preliminary business plan, which I thought was quite generous in terms of royalties to Fabergé. Both he and Perchin were aghast at the idea. 'These are one-of-a-kind creations,' Fabergé said. 'I will not have my vision sullied by mere commerce.' I explained to him, we would be creating just the exterior of the eggs, without the surprises, but he remained adamant.

"You do you know about the 'surprises' inside each egg, Dr. Watson?"

After I admitted to some familiarity, George continued, "In the Blue Serpent Egg, the clock itself was considered the surprise. However, in the Duchess' egg, I understand Fabergé has hidden a tiny music box that plays 'The Nutcracker' by Tchaikovsky. We would have all become very wealthy if only Fabergé had a bit more vision."

I was about to copy the measurements when Georges told me to take the sheet. "That is one dream I fear will never become reality," he said.

After remonstrating with him over his perceived loss, I took my leave and returned to Baker Street, feeling quite pleased with myself. I entered our rooms to find Holmes giving instruction to Wiggins, the nominal leader of the group of street Arabs my friend had dubbed the Baker Street Irregulars.

"And after you've done that, please deliver this letter to Inspector Lestrade and this one to Inspector Hopkins."

As Wiggins turned to leave, Holmes said, "Wait a minute, Wiggins. Watson, so good to see you! Have you procured those things I asked for?"

I nodded in the affirmative and Holmes said, "Splendid! Let me see what you have come up with."

I handed him my paper and he pulled a paper from his the inside pocket of his coat. After he had compared the two, he said "You have done well, Watson."

Holmes then addressed an envelope, placed my sheet of measurements inside and handed it to Wiggins, saying, "After you have visited the Yard, deliver this as addressed. Here's a little something extra for you. I am not expecting any replies, but I may require your services tomorrow."

"You know where to find me, Mr. 'Olmes," replied Wiggins and then he clattered down the stairs and slammed the door as he left.

"Holmes why did you send me on a fool's errand, if you already had the egg's measurements?"

"I am sorry, Watson, but I had to test a theory. To the best of my knowledge, you do not have a larcenous bone in that body, yet you managed to come up with the exact same measurements that I had obtained from the Duchess. The fact that you did it in just a few hours, without resorting to the Duchess, is testament to your determination, and it also makes clear the fact that the egg's dimensions are more commonly known than might have been imagined.

"My point being, if you could obtain them without any undue hardship, so could our Merchant, if he wanted them, and I am inclined to think he does."

"But why? To what end? And to whom was that last letter that you sent addressed?"

"All in due time, Watson. All in due time. And now, I don't know about you but I am absolutely famished, and I have it on good authority that Mrs. Hudson has prepared Welsh rabbit for lunch."

After the meal, which we both thoroughly enjoyed, Holmes said that he had a number of errands to run and to inform Mrs. Hudson he would most likely miss dinner. Left to my own devices, I read and then I spent some time trying to devise exactly how Holmes would bring the Merchant to justice. As you might expect, my efforts were once again unsuccessful.

The next morning, as had become his custom of late, Holmes had departed before I awoke. After I had breakfasted, I took care of several bits of business, including a visit to my tobacconist. I had just returned to Baker Street and was enjoying a solitary lunch when I heard a clatter on the stairs and then three loud knocks on the door. I answered it to find Wiggins standing there.

"I have a letter for Mr. 'Olmes," he said.

"He isn't in," I answered. "You may leave it with me."

The lad shook his head. "No offense, Doctor. I mean I know you are friends with Mr. 'Olmes and all, but I was told to deliver this to him personally and no one else."

"Who told you that?" I asked, feeling a bit put out.

Looking at me curiously, Wiggins replied, "Why the man wot wrote it."

Realizing that I was making no headway, nor was I apt to, I gave the lad tuppence and suggested he return around six.

"Righto, guv," he said, and descended the stairs even more noisily than he had ascended.

When Holmes finally did return around four, I informed him of Wiggins' visit and his refusal to leave the letter with me.

"Now, Watson, don't be annoyed. He was merely following orders. These lads take everything they are told quite literally."

I was sorely tempted to ask whose orders, but I refrained.

And so it was that at exactly six o'clock, I heard the bell, followed by the now familiar sound of Wiggins ascending the stairs. Holmes opened the door before he could pound on it. "This is for you, Mr. 'Olmes," the lad said breathlessly.

"Thank you, Wiggins," said Holmes, slipping the lad a few coins. "In the future, you may feel free to leave any such letters in the care of Dr. Watson."

"Are you sure, sir?" asked the lad.

"Quite! Now off with you." And before the youngster could move, Holmes said, "And you will descend the stairs quietly and refrain from slamming the door."

"Yes, sir," replied Wiggins, who then proceeded to descend the stairs and exit the building as quietly as any sneak thief.

"What is the letter, Holmes?" I asked, after Wiggins had left,

Slitting it open, he perused it at least twice, and then announced, "We should prepare for the Duchess of Marlborough to exhibit her egg on St. George's Day, April 23."

"Why that's little more than two weeks away! Will you be ready in time?"

"I believe I shall be," replied Holmes. "However, just as we are short of time, so too is the Merchant at a similar disadvantage when it comes to formulating his plan to steal the egg."

"You seem certain he will adhere to your calendar," I said.

"I am," said Holmes. "The Duchess has agreed to aid me with a small deception. If the Merchant wishes to secure the Pink Serpent Egg, he must do so at Blenheim or abandon all hope and perhaps make another attempt at one of the Russian royal palaces. And since we will put them on the alert, that rather tips the scales in our favor, does it not?

"Finally, Watson, we are carrying the fight to him. Admittedly, this is not without its risks, but I can see no other way."

"Not without its risks, what on earth do you mean?"

"Well, consider what we know. On those occasions when he was able, he pressured others into committing the crime for him. He threatened Mrs. Sweeney's son. He may have threatened a family member of someone who visited Lady Darbent or Lady Falkland or both. Yet, he participated himself in the attempted theft of the Tara Brooch and in the actual theft at the Louvre."

"And what do you make of that?"

"That anyone who attends the Duchess' gala at Blenheim is a suspect. All of her servants, her guests, even the Duke and Duchess themselves must be viewed with a skeptical eye."

"You can't be serious!"

"I have never been more so," replied Holmes.

Having said that, Holmes then said, "We have a great deal of work to do, and precious little time in which to accomplish it."

"How may I be of assistance?"

"The gathering at Blenheim was to have been a much larger affair, but at Mycroft's insistence, the Duchess has agreed to invite no more than 100 people."

He then handed me a neatly typed list and said, "Here are the names of those expected to be in attendance. If you would be so kind, I would like you to ascertain how many people on the list have small children. That ploy has proved successful for him in the past, and I am inclined to think he may resort to it again."

"Do you really think with all the security that will be in place that any guest would attempt such a brazen act?"

"As you know first-hand, under the proper circumstances, desperate people will commit the most heinous acts. If you can finish that list in the next three days, it would be enormously helpful."

"Yes, but why limit ourselves. After all, couldn't he threaten a man with harming his wife or perhaps his mistress?"

"That thought had crossed my mind. I'm inclined to think a man might simply throttle him were there no great disparity in size. No, Watson, he chooses victims he knows will offer little or no resistance. That also might explain why he was personally involved at both the British Museum and the Louvre. There were no women to threaten."

I mulled over his words and said, "I do believe you may be onto something there. But while I am checking this list, what will you be doing?"

"In the morning, I am off to Blenheim Palace in an effort to make certain that none of the staff there has been suborned."

"I assume you will be going in disguise."

"I rather think so. After all, we will be attending the Duchess' gala, and I wouldn't want anyone to know who we really are before then – especially the servants."

"Who or what will you be this time?"

"I haven't decided just yet. Certainly an itinerant tradesman of some sort. After all, those in service are far more likely to share confidences with a member of their own class. I shall probably be gone before you arise as I intend to get an early train. I expect I shall see you in two or three days if not sooner.

"If any crates should be delivered to Baker Street, please make arrangements to have them forwarded to Blenheim Palace in the care of Mr. Sherlock Holmes."

Knowing that to question him would be fruitless, we turned the conversation to other topics. Holmes was in fine humor, and we enjoyed a rare evening during which we discussed a great many things, and although we did touch on the Merchant, crime was not the focal point of the night. Around ten, Holmes said, "One more pipe before bed, I think."

I declined the offer and decided to turn in. However, I must admit that sleep did not come easily. I was fully aware of exactly what my assignment was, but all I could do was wonder what Holmes might be up to.

Chapter 15

The next morning I awoke to discover there was more than a degree of truth to those April showers about which so many poets have written.

Although my mood was as dark and gray as the skies, I was determined to soldier on. I contacted a friend of mine who worked for The Guardian. Promising a front-page story when all was said and done, he allowed me the use of a desk in his office for as long as needed as well as complete access to the paper's files.

I began by looking into the Duchess of Marlborough. Although I had heard she was rather young, I was surprised to learn that she was, in fact, only 25 and her husband, but 31. The Duchess, who was a mere 18 when she wed, was now the mother of 5-year-old John Spencer-Churchill and 4-year-old Ivor Spencer-Churchill, the former of whom would someday become the 10th Duke of Marlborough. I wondered if the Merchant were brazen enough to try to intimidate the Duchess by threatening her sons.

As I continued my efforts, it soon became evident that the majority of their acquaintances, close and otherwise, were considerably older. I wondered how well the Duchess, younger and an American, got along with her blue-blood friends. Something told me she was an outlier, and I thought, because she was, she might be perceived as vulnerable.

Over the course of the next two days, I worked my way through the list of names, checking family connections while focusing on any and all offspring under the age of 10. Admittedly, it was an arbitrary choice, but I had to draw the line somewhere. As I trudged home after the first day, it dawned upon me that much of my labor could have been accomplished much more quickly had I been allowed to confide in my friend at the paper.

Nevertheless, Holmes had asked for secrecy and I knew how important that could be to whatever plan he might be devising.

After dinner, I decided I deserved a treat and opened a bottle of cognac I had been saving for some time. It proved the perfect antidote to an otherwise dreary, tiresome day.

I returned to my task the next morning, and by noon, I had checked every name on the list Holmes had given me. I was rather surprised when I tallied things up to discover that besides the Duchess, only seven other women on the list had children younger than 10.

I lunched at my club and spent the rest of the afternoon taking care of a few errands. When I returned to Baker Street around five, I found Holmes in a familiar position, sitting in his chair, fingers steepled under his chin, deep in thought.

"I must say that I am surprised to see you here. I can only assume your endeavors proved successful."

"Things could not have gone better," he replied. "By the way, Watson, your description of Blenheim was most helpful."

"How on Earth did you get to see Blenheim? On my visit, I had the distinct impression that visitors, especially unexpected ones, were most unwelcome. Even though I was expected, I would still describe my reception there as rather chilly, bordering on frigid."

Holmes laughed heartily. "Thank you, Watson. I needed a bit of levity."

"I suppose they welcomed you with open arms."

"No, but I was welcomed, and rather warmly I might add."

"Do tell?"

"I must admit, Watson, to indulging in a bit of deception to ensure my warm welcome. However, I was quite prepared to resort to another bit of subterfuge, had my initial effort proved unsuccessful."

"You mean you had two plans to gain entrance to Blenheim?"

"Watson, you should know by now that I never approach any situation with only one arrow in my quiver. Truth be told, I had three separate plans to gain access to Blenheim; fortunately, as I said, there was no need to resort to the other two."

"And what master stroke allowed you to gain entrance to the palace?"

"At the last minute, I decided to change my disguise and thus I arrived at the front door with a box of books which I said His Lordship had ordered for the library. After I had waited some few minutes in the Main Hall, I was escorted past the Main Salon and into the Long Library. Incidentally, Watson, I think I should much prefer the Duchess display her egg in that room. After examining the volumes on the shelves – by the way, given the dust that has accumulated on the tops of the books at which I looked – I am inclined to think the Duke's books are purely decorative. When I had finished my examination of the room, I placed several of the books on the various shelves, rearranged a number of others and informed Childers that I would no doubt be returning in the near future with additional volumes.

"He then invited me to the kitchen for lunch and, like you, I was treated to a tour although mine was rather brief by comparison. It is a remarkable estate, Watson. Perhaps instead of chronicling my exploits, you should focus one of your literary efforts on the rich history of that grand manse."

"Perhaps, I shall someday. At any rate, if your book gambit had not worked, what then were you planning to do?"

"In the bottom of the case in which I carried the books, I had fashioned a compartment similar to that of the bag the Merchant had provided Mrs. Sweeney."

"To what end? You weren't planning on pilfering anything were you?"

"No! Quite the contrary. If required, I was planning to introduce something."

"What? Pray tell."

"I had placed three large mice in the compartment. If necessary, they might have found a temporary home at Blenheim Palace. At any rate, they would certainly have needed a rat-catcher there, and I was prepared to return in an entirely different disguise a bit later and introduce myself as Tom Black, son of the late royal rat-catcher, Jack Black."

"Holmes, you astound me. Are there no lengths to which you will not resort?"

"To see this Merchant captured, there is precious little I would not do. In fact, I had even ventured so far as to pack a pair of white leather breeches, a scarlet waistcoat, a green topcoat, a hat with a gold band around it, and a sash emblazoned with metal rat-shaped medallions."

"My word, that is his costume right down to the medals."

"I have used it in the past, and I have no doubt that I shall don it again in the future."

"Since Tom Black is so well known, aren't you running a bit of a risk?"

"Believe me, Watson, people are willing to trust just about anyone who says he can render their homes free of mice and other vermin. And you can be certain, the staff members at Blenheim are no exception."

"Yes, yes, I see that now. So you found out what you needed to know?"

"My second day there, I donned a different disguise, and I was fortunate to encounter one of the maids on her day off at the market in Oxford. After striking up a conversation, I escorted her to one of the local public houses for dinner, and, I must say, after several glasses of wine, she proved quite informative. She vouched for each of the staff members. Apparently, they all love the Duchess and her children; however, the Duke is another matter.

"They have all been with the family in various capacities for at least five years, and they are all treated quite well. Moreover, none of them has left Blenheim for more than a day or two in the last six months as they have all been involved to some degree with the restoration work, which is being carried out under the ever-watchful eye of the Duke.

"I think we can eliminate the servants as a source of consternation. Which means I must now focus our attention primarily on the guests and anyone else who might be brought in to serve at the gala."

"Speaking of which," I said, "I checked all the names on that list you gave me, and only seven women, not including the Duchess, have young children."

"Ah yes, the Duchess," mused Holmes, "I was aware that she had two young sons, which is something we must bear in mind going forward." Rising from his chair, he looked about, "I see the crate I was expecting has not yet arrived."

"Although there have been two cables and several letters delivered for you, there have been no packages of any kind," I said.

"Excellent," he said. Sitting at the dinner table, he composed a short note, placed it in an envelope and sealed it. Throwing open the window, he emitted a high-pitched whistle and a few minutes later, I heard a familiar clatter on the stairs, followed by three quick raps on the door.

"Come in, Wiggins," said Holmes. Immediately the door was opened by the head of the Irregulars. "What can I do for you, Mr. 'Olmes?"

Holmes handed him the letter, saying, "When you deliver this letter, please say that Mr. Holmes says, 'All the instructions are to be followed to the letter.' And here is the address for the delivery. When it is delivered, tell him to have his man inform the butler, Childers, that the Duke and Mr. Chambers would like the crate placed in the library. They will unpack it when they arrive.

"One final thing, tell him I need the crate delivered to Blenheim as soon as possible. See if he can give you a date when he plans to ship it. Have you got all that?"

"Yes sir," replied the lad.

Despite the boy's assurance, Holmes made him repeat the instructions back to him, which the youngster did word for word. After handing him a few coins, Holmes said, "Off with you now. And mind the door."

Although he made as much noise going down the stairs as he had coming up, he did leave without slamming the door.

"What was that all about?"

"Just a little something I am having delivered to the Long Library at Blenheim."

"And who is this Mr. Chambers?"

Holmes chuckled, "I am, of course, in my guise as a bookseller extraordinaire."

"Is the Duke aware of your doings," I inquired.

"To a degree," replied Holmes. "As I said, Mycroft contacted him and asked for his help in capturing this Merchant. When he mentioned the new Fabergé egg might be at risk, the Duke was more than happy to cooperate. After all, I should think the promise of the government reimbursing him for the cost of the egg should ensure his cooperation with few, if any, questions asked."

"And has he cooperated?"

"Thus far, he has been as good as his word."

"I would dearly love to know what you are planning," I said.

"And eventually you shall, Watson." said Holmes. "I do not enjoy keeping you in the dark, my friend, but a wrong glance, an inadvertent gasp or a telltale reaction at an inopportune moment could undermine this entire construct. And besides, how else can I indulge in my flair for the dramatic which you have so often pointed out?"

Under other circumstances, I might have been cross with Holmes and what I initially perceived as his mistrust of me, but then I recalled the words that I had spoken to him on one occasion – "I am not nearly so deft a dissembler as you" – and I realized he was correct in his assessment.

"Trust me, Watson, before this affair is concluded, you will have a significant role to play."

I couldn't tell if Holmes were merely trying to assuage my bruised feelings or if he were telling the truth, but I decided to take him at his word.

"By the way, Watson, Mrs. Hudson had a family emergency, so we will have to fend for ourselves when it comes to dinner tonight."

"Nothing serious, I hope."

"She did not seem terribly upset, so I am going to assume perhaps it is a relative fallen ill. At any rate, if you're in the mood for seafood, I will treat you to dinner at Wilton's in recognition of your two days of dogged detective work."

Easily one of the best seafood restaurants in London as well as laying claim to be being the city's oldest eatery, I knew dinner at Wilton's was going to cost my friend a pretty penny."

"That is really not necessary, Holmes," I said. "Besides, it almost sounds as though we are celebrating, and you are never one to act prematurely."

"True, enough, Watson. Think of this more as a well-deserved diversion than a celebration."

"Well, if you insist." I must admit that the prospect of a delightful meal made me a rather willing accomplice.

"Come Watson, you are as fond of oysters as I am, and after we have eaten, perhaps a nightcap at the Diogenes Club? I have one or two things to discuss with Mycroft."

"Oh, so it is business and pleasure," I laughed.

"Isn't it always?" replied Holmes.

Minutes earlier, I had been feeling out of sorts because of a perceived slight, and now all was right with the world as I felt Holmes had recognized my worth. What a strange relationship we have, I thought to myself.

On our way to the restaurant and throughout dinner, Holmes was quite jovial, and the Chablis that he selected was certainly a fine one.

After dinner, we hailed a cab and Holmes told the driver to take us to the Diogenes Club.

When we arrived, we were led into the Stranger's Room to await Mycroft. A moment later, a valet appeared, carrying a silver tray with a letter upon it. "Mr. Holmes was called back to office," he explained, "but he said that I should present this to you as soon as you arrived."

Holmes took the letter, broke the wax seal and pulled out a single sheet of paper that had been folded in half. He perused it carefully. After thanking the valet, he looked at me and said simply, "Mycroft has come through once again. He informs me that the Duchess has requested a meeting tomorrow at noon at Marlborough House. If you are free, would you care to accompany me?"

"Do you have any idea why she wants to meet?" I asked.

"I can only surmise she has heard of our involvement and perhaps has important information she wishes to impart."

"Do you really believe that?"

"No, Watson, I fear the Duchess has a far more personal reason for requesting a face-to-face meeting, but speculating about it is futile. So, as we have done so often in this case, let us wait patiently for the morrow, and then we will know for certain."

The next morning after breakfast, Holmes immersed himself in the papers, paying no mind to the time. Finally, about 11:30, I said, "Don't you think we should be on our way?"

"I suppose so," replied my friend, and a few minutes later, we were in a cab headed for the grand estate in St. James' Square.

When we arrived, we were led into a sitting room by a servant in livery. Although Marlborough House pales in comparison to Blenheim, it is still quite something to see. Until recently, it had been the residence of King Edward VII, who had abandoned it for Buckingham Palace after the passing of his mother, Queen Victoria.

We were waiting but a few moments, and Holmes was prowling about the room as is his wont. Suddenly, the door opened and a stunning young woman entered. She was tall and slim with an oval face perched upon a long slender neck. I was captivated by her enormous dark eyes, but I could see that she was troubled by something.

Looking first at Holmes and then at me, she returned her gaze to Holmes and said in a pronounced American accent, "Mister Holmes, thank God you have come. I am afraid that you are the only one who can save me." And with that she burst into tears.

Chapter 16

I rushed to the woman, pulling my handkerchief from my pocket as I did so. Leading her to a divan, I sat beside her and attempted to reassure her, "Now, now, my dear. If you have a problem, you can rest assured Sherlock Holmes is more than capable of solving it."

Looking up at Holmes, she said through her tears, "Can you help me, Mister Holmes? I have heard such wonderful things about you."

Speaking softly to the distraught woman, Holmes replied simply, "Your Ladyship, every case is different, but I give you my word, I shall do all in my power to alleviate your distress."

Holmes' words seemed to ease her fears somewhat. Gathering herself, she stood and said, "Where are my manners? I am Consuelo Vanderbilt. Please, when we are alone, call me Consuelo? I am not one to stand on formality."

"I shall do my best," replied Holmes, "but having been raised in a certain manner, I fear that is one request I may not be able to honor."

She smiled at his remark, and I could see her relax just the slightest bit. "Would you care for some refreshment?" she asked.

"Perhaps after we have finished our meeting," said Holmes. "Right now, I would like you to tell us about the threat to your sons."

To say the woman was stunned would be the grossest of understatements. "How could you possibly know?" she gasped. "I have told no one, not even my husband."

Holmes looked at her and uttered a line I had heard him use before, "Madam, I am Sherlock Holmes. It is my business to know what other people do not."

"So what they say about you is true," she replied. "Last week while out shopping, I was accosted by a man in Harrods. He came up to me and in a very familiar tone inquired, 'Consuelo? Consuelo Vanderbilt? You may not remember me, but I'm Hamilton Fish. I am a business partner of your father's in New York.'"

Holmes merely sniffed. Picking up on the sudden change in his mood, the Duchess inquired, "What's wrong Mr. Holmes?"

"I'm sensing a familiar stratagem here. The man you met was obviously an American."

"Oh yes," she replied. "He had a very distinct accent, but he was not from New York. Of that, I am certain. What did you mean about a familiar stratagem?"

"This man you met employs a variety of aliases, most of which appear to be taken from the Cabinets of your presidents. Hamilton Fish served as Secretary of State under Ulysses Grant."

"Oh my word," she exclaimed. "So he has done this sort of thing before?"

"Too many times," replied Holmes, "and I am determined to put an end to his reign of terror over you and other women in your position. Now tell me about the threats he made against your sons."

The Duchess then related how the man had invited her to tea and from that point on her tale seemed like a recitation of the story that Mrs. Sweeney had related to Holmes. When she had finished, she said, "Since you know so much, Mr. Holmes, I suppose you are aware that my marriage to the Duke was arranged. I was bought and sold like so much chattel. Do you know that your newspapers often refer to me as a 'dollar princess'? Be that as it may, although I do not love my husband, my boys are my world.

"Shortly after our marriage, I was informed by the Duke that my primary duty was to produce an heir. Well, I have done my duty twice over," she said. "In fact, my husband is wont to say that I gave him 'an heir and a spare.' Those are our children, Mr. Holmes, and Sunny speaks of them in that manner."

"Sunny?" I inquired.

"Unless I am much mistaken, Sunny is a nickname stemming from the Duke's other title, the Earl of Sunderland."

"You really are well-informed, Mr. Holmes."

Deftly changing the subject, Holmes asked, "What did this man say about the Fabergé egg?"

"The man I met wanted me to get it and leave it in this very room that night. I told him such a thing was impossible as the egg was being held in a bank vault only my husband could

162

access. He then asked if I planned to display the egg at some point in the future.

"I told him plans were being made to show the egg at Blenheim Palace. When I informed him that the entire affair was being arranged by my husband, he instructed me to provide him with all of the details as soon as I learned them."

"Excellent," remarked Holmes. "How are you to communicate with him?'

"I am to place a personal in the agony column of The Daily Mail. The ad should request a meeting on the date when the egg is to be displayed. It should also include the hours when it will be on display and the room in which it is to be shown.

"He told me if I did that, I would have done all that I could, and my boys would be safe."

"Madam, trust me. Even if you were to follow his instructions to the letter, he might well make additional demands, but for now, let us accede to his wishes and see what transpires."

"He did say one other thing, Mr. Holmes. He told me you might contact me, and if you did, I was to inform you this is none of your affair. He also said that if he saw you anywhere near where the egg is to be displayed, he could not be held responsible for his own actions."

"That is outrageous!" I exclaimed. "He seeks to break the law with impunity. It is as though he were asking us to commit a sin of omission."

"I had rather anticipated those few demands, Watson," said Holmes. Turning to the Duchess, he continued, "As I said, we have dealt with this man before. He is quite clever, and as you can see, he has anticipated our involvement. However, you have nothing to fear. If you would be so kind as to add a Dr. Johnson and a Michael Wigstrom to the guest list at Blenheim that would be a tremendous help. You may rest assured Dr. Watson and I will both be there, but we will, in all likelihood, be disguised so there is little chance of his recognizing us."

I could see that the Duchess wanted to believe Holmes, but that she still harbored reservations.

Sensing her anxiety, Holmes said, "Madam, I can understand and appreciate your fear, but the only way for this to be truly over for you is for us to apprehend the man behind the threats. You do see that?

"Today, he demands your Fabergé egg in exchange for your sons' safety. Perhaps in two years or five, he returns requesting something else you have acquired. People like this Merchant, as Watson has taken to calling him, are little more than bullies at heart. They threaten and they take what they want. However, I will grant you this, he is a most dangerous adversary, and that is why we must end his career now."

After pausing a bit, the Duchess looked at Holmes and said softly, "I have been ordered about my entire life. First, by my mother, who forced me to wed, and then by my husband. And now by this Merchant. I am sick and tired of it. I will help you Mister Holmes because I think it is time I begin to stand up for myself."

I know I was touched by the woman's blunt honesty, and I think in some small way, it affected my friend as well.

"Excellent," said Holmes. "I commend your courage. Now here is what we must do." Holmes then set about helping to draft the advertisement that would run in The Daily Mail. As the writer in the group, it fell to me to do the actual composing, and while I did offer some small input, the bulk of the planning was actually carried out by the Duchess and Holmes.

However, when they were about halfway through, I did manage to make one significant contribution. "Why not run the advertisement tomorrow saying that plans for the meeting are still being finalized and then run the second advertisement on the Monday prior. That way he will have very little time to plan while we will have stolen a march of several days."

"Bravo, Watson. An excellent suggestion!"

I was delighted to have helped my friend and the Duchess. For those who might be interested, I have reproduced our efforts – just as they appeared in print – below.

The first one read:

The meeting is still being arranged. Will convey all details as soon

as they become available, possibly on Monday.

While the second one, scheduled to run a few days later, was far more businesslike and to the point.

Meeting to begin at 7 p.m. on 23 April
in the Long Library of the Palace.

Business will be conducted until midnight.
The guest list will meet all of your specifications.

As we were preparing to leave, Holmes turned to the Duchess and said, "I have but one more question for you?"

"Yes?"

"When you took possession of the Fabergé egg, how was it packed?"

"Oh, Mister Fabergé had designed a special box for transporting the egg. The outside is made of lacquered wood and his insignia has been carved into it, and the inside is lined with plush red velvet. Behind the velvet is some sort of soft material, perhaps cotton. So the egg is both protected and cushioned."

"Excellent," replied Holmes. "And the box is about the same dimensions as the egg, though slightly larger to accommodate it?"

"Exactly," said the Duchess. "It made it all the way here from Russia without any sort of mishap. Is that important?"

"It may be," replied Holmes. "That has yet to be determined."

When we finally took our leave, I could see the Duchess was in a much better frame of mind. Holmes had promised her the boys would be safe and they would be under constant, albeit unobtrusive, surveillance. He also instructed her to refrain from shopping alone and, if possible, to remain on the grounds of Marlborough House until certain additions had been made to the staff. Finally, Holmes also informed her that if the need were to arise, she should feel free to contact us at any time, day or night, at Baker Street.

When we left, I asked, "How are you going to protect those boys? You're not going to ask the Irregulars to watch over them?"

"Absolutely not," replied my friend, "I am going to task Mycroft with that responsibility. I am certain the addition of two new men to a staff of that size would hardly be noticed."

"I assume I am going to be Dr. Johnson at the Blenheim gala."

"Absolutely," replied Holmes. "You have been my Boswell for so long that I think it high time you essayed the role of Dr. Johnson."

"Splendid," I laughed, "but what if someone should recognize me?"

"Well, you can go in disguise, or you can simply tell them you desired an evening without Sherlock Holmes, which will explain my perceived absence and the alias. Should anyone ask, simply say you were hoping to avoid telling the tales you have told so many times before. If you are pressed to detail our exploits, well, I leave that decision to you."

"Splendid," I replied, "but who the deuce is Michael Wigstrom?"

"The Merchant has no monopoly on this name game, Watson. Two of Fabergé's best craftsmen are Michael Perchin and Henrik Wigstrom. I thought of just using Perchin, but on the chance that he might recognize that name, I decided to simply combine them into an innocuous third name.

"Well, the Duchess didn't seem to recognize it." I said.

"Exactly," he replied.

By now we had reached Marlborough Road, and we stood there for some few minutes waiting for a cab to appear. When one finally did, Holmes hailed it, and as we were about to climb in, he turned to me, and speaking rather loudly I thought, said, "You know, Watson, the more I think about it, the angrier I become. That woman is so obstinate I have decided to wash my hands of this case."

As we started down the street, I said to Holmes, "Pray tell, what was that bit of histrionics all about?"

"You are not going to tell me you failed to observe him?"

"Observe whom?"

"The boy who has been following us ever since we left Baker Street. Perhaps 13 or 14, tall and thin with a shock of dark hair. He was wearing brown knickers, a blue shirt and with a brown jacket and cap. I noticed him loitering outside our rooms when we left earlier. His appearance here could not be coincidence."

"What are you saying?"

"I believe that the Merchant has emulated my methods by recruiting his own band of street Arabs to keep watch over us and report our comings and goings."

"So that bluster about washing your hands …"

"Was all for the benefit of the Merchant," replied Holmes. "I am certain the boy will report what he heard, though I doubt it will do much good. Still, it may give our adversary pause for a moment."

When we returned to Baker Street, Wiggins was waiting for us at the door. "Mr. 'Olmes, I gave that bloke your message. He says everything will be taken care of by Monday, and 'e's 'avin' it delivered to that country 'ouse, just as you requested."

"Thank you, Wiggins," replied Holmes. He then slipped the boy a note. Before he could scamper off, Holmes said, "I have one more assignment for you and the lads, Wiggins."

Holmes then explained that he wanted Wiggins and his companions to see if anyone else were hiring youngsters to do what the Irregulars did. "You can say that you are looking for better wages as the assignments from me have dried up." He made a point of instructing Wiggins that if he discovered anything, he should report to Holmes at once. As the lad turned, Holmes said, "One more thing, Wiggins. Do be careful. We are dealing with a very bad man, here, so tread lightly."

Wiggins just laughed and said, "Not to worry, Mr. 'Olmes. I'll be so quiet, they won't even know I was asking." I watched as he then sprinted off in the direction of Marylebone Road.

Turning back to Holmes, I asked, "Are you sure that was wise?"

"I must admit that I am not keen on involving the Irregulars, but what choice do I have? You and I cannot pose the questions that need to be asked and neither can the Yard. Besides, I trust Wiggins to come up with a plausible story should the need arise."

When we had ascended to our rooms, there were two letters and a cable waiting for Holmes. He read them, composed replies and then dashed off two other notes. Finally he called for Billy, the page, and instructed him: "After you have sent these two cables, please deliver this note to my brother, Mycroft, at the Diogenes Club; and this one to Inspector Lestrade."

"Yes sir," said the lad, who then clattered down the stairs as loudly as though he were Wiggins' twin.

"Do you think it wise to involve Lestrade in your plans while you keep them secret from me?" I sniffed.

"Only to the extent that I must," he replied. "It is necessary to take Lestrade into our confidence. After all, someone has to arrest this Merchant and take him into custody. Given our lack of legal standing, it certainly can't be you or me."

Although I was still slightly miffed at not knowing what Holmes had planned, I reasoned Lestrade would make excellent company – in the dark.

That evening, perhaps an hour after we had finished dining, I heard the bell ring. Holmes glanced at his watch and said, "That will be Lestrade." And then I heard the good Inspector's rather heavy footfalls as he climbed the stairs. His soft knock was greeted with, "Do come in, Inspector. You are just in time to join Watson and me in an after-dinner brandy."

Settling himself into one of the wing chairs, Lestrade said, "Don't mind if I do Mr. Holmes. I can tell you, it has been one thing after another lately, and would you believe that I still hear from Lord Thornton occasionally about his missing knife."

"His *jambiya*," corrected Holmes gently. "And that's exactly why I have called you here. I require your assistance."

Perking up, Lestrade looked at Holmes quizzically and said, "Did I hear you right, Mr. Holmes? You need my help?"

"Indeed, I do," replied Holmes. "I believe that I am getting very close to apprehending the man who stole Thornton's *jambiya*, as well as committed any number of other crimes both here and abroad. However, to bring him to justice, I believe your cooperation is imperative."

"If you can free me from Lord Thornton, then I am your man," said Lestrade.

"Here is what I hope will happen," said Holmes. He then explained about the Duchess of Marlborough's egg, the gala at Blenheim, and his plan to lure the Merchant to the palace by means of the agony columns.

"And just what do you need me for?" asked Lestrade. "It sounds as though you have everything under control."

"You must be on the scene, so that when he does try to make off with the egg, you can arrest him. The rest of the charges will fall into place after that. You have experience with this sort of thing, and I am certain the local constabulary does not, which is why I am loath to involve them."

"Well, we might be stepping on a few toes, jurisdictionally speaking, but if it brings this blackguard to justice, we can always issue apologies afterwards and send some of the credit their way, I suppose."

"Exactly. Far better to ask forgiveness than permission, I always say," replied Holmes.

At that the three of us laughed, knowing how often Holmes had walked that fine line. And then my friend continued, "Yes, this will require a degree of cooperation, but for the moment, that compact is limited to the people in this room."

"Exactly, what is it you would have me do, Mr. Holmes?"

"I need you and one of your best men to be on hand at the gala at Blenheim Palace next Wednesday."

"Blenheim Palace," said Lestrade with more than a bit of awe in his voice. "I must say you are moving in high society, Mr. Holmes. What exactly will you be expecting from us?"

Holmes then outlined everything that he was counting on from Lestrade, who seemed quite relieved when Holmes had finished. "That's really all we need do to capture this Merchant?" asked Lestrade.

"If all goes according to plan, yes. Sadly, things can go awry, but as Watson will tell you, I always have at least two other plans in place, should that happen."

"Well, let's hope we have no need of those other plans," said Lestrade, who then rose to leave. "So unless I hear from you otherwise, my man and I will be at Blenheim next Wednesday evening."

"I think we should meet one more time before then," said Holmes. "I will notify you about the particulars and any alterations to my plans."

"I will wait to hear from you," said Lestrade, who then took his leave.

I had to admit that I felt somewhat better after the inspector had departed. Holmes hadn't told him anything that I didn't know, and in fact, in one or two areas, I knew somewhat more than the inspector. Moreover, as it turned out, I would have a larger role to play.

Looking at me, Holmes smiled and said, "I can see that you are feeling better. Perhaps a pipe and another brandy."

"That sounds splendid. What is your next move, Holmes?"

"I must rise early and make another trip to Blenheim Palace as Mister Chambers. I need to install a few more books in the Duke's burgeoning library and then I must make certain that the room is arranged just so. You know what they say, Watson: 'A place for everything, and everything in its place.'

"It is imperative I control those things I can, and hope for the best in the remaining areas. But the room is key. Everything has to be spot on."

Of course, I had no idea what Holmes was talking about, and I thought to myself, "Good luck in trying to manage that room." I remembered Childers, the butler at Blenheim, telling me that the Long Library was believed to be the second longest room in any house in England. Keeping things under control was going to be a Herculean task, but then I reflected on everything Holmes had accomplished over his illustrious career, and I felt certain that if anyone could manage such a situation, it would be he.

As we smoked and talked, I little realized the peril that lay before us. If I had, I think I might have tried to savor every moment of that evening.

Chapter 17

As always, Holmes was as good as his word. When I awoke the next morning, I was greeted by a note on the table that read:

Watson,

> *I have taken the early train to Blenheim. I will be in touch. Do pick up copies of all the papers and hold them for me. Also, check to see that the Duchess' personal appears in The Daily Mail.*

> *S.H.*

I sent the buttons out for the morning papers, and there in The Mail was the advertisement from the Duchess, advising that the meeting was still in the planning stages. With nothing clamoring for my immediate attention, I spent the next hour or so enjoying several cups of coffee and perusing the papers.

I must admit to being taken aback when I came across a piece in the society column in The Times about the upcoming gala at Blenheim. The article discussed not only the Fabergé egg in some detail, but it also included the time as well a number of the notables who had been invited. "Holmes is not going to be pleased when he learns of this," I thought.

I believed I was looking at a long, tedious day when I heard the bell ring. The page soon knocked on the door, and when I bade him enter, he brought me a note. A friend, Dr. Harrell, had been called away to Sussex by a family emergency. He was hoping I might cover his practice for the rest of the day, and possibly Saturday. I quickly scribbled a reply, and began to gather my things. It seemed like an excellent way to fill the time in Holmes' absence.

I returned late that night, bolted down a cold platter that Mrs. Hudson had left for me and threw myself into bed. I awoke the next morning and returned to Harrell's practice, which I had agreed to cover until midday, as it was a Saturday. As I made my way back to Baker Street, it suddenly dawned upon me that Holmes' intended tete-a-tete with the Merchant was now less than a week away.

I opened the door and was surprised to see Holmes, sitting in his chair, playing his violin. "You are home already?"

"Yes, things went quite smoothly at Blenheim. I plan to return to the palace Tuesday night, and then quite obviously again Wednesday afternoon, but things have fallen into place quite nicely."

"Will you spend Tuesday night in Oxford?"

"I suppose so," he replied, "but it is too soon to say with absolute certainty."

"Speaking of Blenheim, the paper is there with the Duchess' personal in the agony column, but the cat may have got out of the bag."

"Oh, you mean the article about the gala with all the particulars that appeared on the society page of the Times?"

"You know about it?"

"Of course, I do. I arranged for its placement."

"But why? I thought we had agreed that such notice would allow the Merchant more time to plan."

"And so we did. Watson. Did you read the article carefully or merely glance at it?"

I had to admit that I was so surprised to see it that I hadn't given it my undivided attention.

"I thought so," laughed Holmes. "Well, had you read the article a bit more carefully, you might have noticed one or two differences between what the article says is going to happen and what we hope will actually occur."

"Are they significant?"

"I should say so," said Holmes. "For one thing, the article says the egg will be displayed in the Main Salon, but as you and I know, the egg can be seen only by visiting the Long Library."

"So you deliberately supplied The Times with false information?"

"Guilty as charged," laughed my friend. "This entire plan depends upon a bit of misinformation and to some degree misdirection. There, I have said enough. You now know more than the Merchant, Watson. See if you can anticipate my movements."

I knew trying to get my friend to divulge anything further was fruitless, so I sat in my chair and reviewed everything I had learned thus far. I must have dozed off because my reverie was suddenly interrupted by the doorbell. A few minutes later, Mrs. Hudson knocked on the door.

"Yes, Mrs. Hudson?" said Holmes.

"A package for you, Mr. Holmes."

At that, Holmes went to the door, opened it, and took a small wooden crate from our landlady. Thanking her, he turned and placed the box on the dinner table.

"What have you got there, Holmes?" I asked.

He smiled and replied, "This is the last piece of the puzzle."

"Well, aren't we being secretive," I said.

"If you must know, it's a box."

"I can see that," I replied. "What is inside the box?"

"A glass dome, such as might be used for an anniversary clock."

"Obviously, this has something to do with the Duchess' egg."

"Yes, this is a very special dome that I have had made. This will allow her to display the egg in relative safety. The glass will prevent curious fingers from touching it and possibly damaging it."

"There's more to it than that," I said. "I have never known you to be that altruistic."

"As I said earlier, Watson, you know more than the Merchant. Try to think like him. How would you steal the egg? Then try to imagine yourself in my shoes. What can you do to foil his plan? Consider it a variant of chess. I must admit such ruminations have often provided me with hours of pleasure."

With that, he picked up the box and carried it to his bedroom. As he reached the door, he turned to me and said, "I have supplied you with ample information. It remains for you to assemble the disparate pieces into a cohesive whole. Shall we dine at six? And then possibly take in a special advance performance of *Rigoletto* at the Royal Opera House. They have this promising young tenor – Enrico Caruso is his name, I believe – who seems to be the talk of the town."

"But *Rigoletto* is not scheduled to open until next month," I said.

"True, however, this is a performance for patrons of the theatre. The Duchess had no interest in attending, and she was kind enough to ask if I might be."

"Holmes, you are incorrigible. I would be delighted to attend. As you said, this Caruso is the current wunderkind. I can only hope that his talent is even somewhat close to his burgeoning reputation."

"Well, there is but one way to find out."

That night is one I will always cherish. Caruso not only lived up to his reputation, he exceeded it. Performing on a bare stage, with just a few lights and fewer props, Caruso brought the Duke of Mantua to life. Performing opposite him was the Australian soprano, Nellie Melba, who at that time was Covent Garden's highest-paid diva.

As you might expect, Holmes and I both promised ourselves we would return to see the fully staged version of the opera.

As it turned out, it was also the last tranquil night we would spend together for some time. Truth be told, that night really was the calm before the storm – a storm that nearly ended in tragedy for Holmes and myself.

On Sunday, Holmes was out most of the day, returning in the evening carrying a long cylindrical tube under his arm and a look of quiet determination on his countenance. I managed to refrain from asking any questions, and finally he broke the silence, saying, "I hope it is not an imposition, but I have asked Lestrade and his man to stop by later this evening so that we might have one final briefing and coordinate our activities at Blenheim."

"Not an imposition at all," I replied. I was grateful at having been included in the plans although I had yet to determine my exact role.

The hours seemed interminable, but finally at around 9 p.m., I heard the bell ring and two sets of footsteps ascending the stairs. I recognized Lestrade's knock, and Holmes said, "Come in, Inspector."

A moment later, Lestrade entered, followed by a rugged looking young man who looked to be in his mid-30s. He was quite tall, well over six feet, and looked to be an imposing physical specimen. "Mr. Holmes, Dr. Watson, this is PC Richard Lawless. He's a rising star at the Yard, Mr. Holmes, and I think he may soon be looking at my job."

The young man nearly blushed, and Lestrade chuckled when he noticed. He looked at his fellow officer and said, "If things turn out the way they usually do with Mr. Holmes, this could prove to be quite a feather in your cap."

"Lawless, that is quite the name for a member of Scotland Yard," I observed.

"I have heard that before," he replied with a big grin.

My attempt at humor elicited a slight grimace from Holmes, but the young constable seemed unfazed.

"I cannot thank you enough, Inspector, and you as well, Mr. Holmes."

"Let us see if you are still thanking me Wednesday night," said Holmes. "I will be back momentarily," he added. He then stepped into his room and returned with the tube he had brought home earlier that day.

"What have you got there, Mr. Holmes?" asked Lestrade.

Extracting a long rolled-up sheet from the tube, Holmes said, "This is a detailed drawing of the Long Library and the rooms and grounds immediately surrounding it at Blenheim Palace. As you may or may not know, it is one of the longest rooms in any English estate.

"The Long Library measures approximately 16 feet wide by nearly 150 feet long, hence the name. At one end is a large statue of Queen Anne on a pedestal, which I am told is a rather flattering depiction of Her Highness."

We all chuckled at Holmes' remark, but he seemed not to notice. "At the other end is an enormous Willis organ that was built and installed just about a decade ago. I do not know if the Duchess has found an accomplished organist, so the question of music remains up in the air at the moment."

Pointing to a spot on the map, Holmes said, "You will notice, there is but a single entrance to the room, which is one of the reasons I selected it for this encounter. The exterior wall is made up of a series of windows, while the interior wall is lined with bookcases which the Duke is in the process of filling. Should the Merchant attempt to escape, he will either have to make his way back through the palace or break one of the windows and hope for the best.

"Opposite the single entrance is a rather large alcove; however, it will be blocked off by a large Coromandel screen that the Duke picked up in his travels. So we need not concern ourselves with that. In front of that screen will be placed a small table on which the Fabergé egg will be displayed under a glass dome."

"I can see that you have put a fair amount of planning into this," said Lestrade. "What exactly will you be wanting Lawless and me to do?"

"Ah, Inspector. At the moment, I plan on having you attend the party as a guest. It is formal attire, by the way. During the evening, I want you to keep watch on the windows to the left of the alcove," said Holmes. Looking at me, he said, "Watson, you are to keep watch on the remaining windows."

"But why am I at this party?" asked Lestrade. "I'm just a copper, not a swell."

"Yes, but on Wednesday morning, you and Constable Lawless are going to accompany the Duke to his bank and then act as his bodyguards as he travels to Blenheim. His Lordship is going to be so pleased with your attentiveness that he is going to insist that you stay for the gala and continue to watch over the egg."

"So people will know I'm from Scotland Yard," asked Lestrade.

"Of course," said Holmes. "You can regale the guests by telling them stories of all the cases we have worked on together."

At that, Lestrade cast a wry glance at Holmes, who merely smiled.

"And me, Mr. Holmes?" asked Lawless.

"Ah, yes. Unfortunately, I am going to require you to conceal yourself in the bushes beneath the alcove windows for several hours. That way you can quickly sprint to either side, should you be needed. It will be a long, tedious night, I'm afraid, but yours is a key role. You may be the first to see the Merchant should he attempt to break in, and if he should escape, it may well fall to you to capture him."

"I will not let you down, sir," said Lawless.

"And where will you be, Mr. Holmes?" asked Lestrade.

"Oh, I will be around, Lestrade," said Holmes lightly. "You can be certain of that, and if you do not see me, do not concern yourself. Trust me when I say, I will be there."

"I think I know what that means," said Lestrade, casting a glance my way.

"I rather doubt it," retorted Holmes, "but we shall see."

Turning back to me, Holmes said, "Watson, the Duchess is expecting you to arrive Wednesday morning. She was kind enough to set aside a room for you. I shall probably be there when you arrive, but if you should see me, do not acknowledge me in any way. And if you should fail to see me, you need not be concerned. There are still a few details which I must finalize."

"I assume that I should ignore you as well, Mr. Holmes?" asked Lestrade.

"Yes," replied Holmes. "We need to be as inconspicuous as possible while we are there. Make every attempt to blend in, but keep your wits about you at all time."

Holmes then went over all the instructions a second time. "There will be no dress rehearsal," he said. "This is our best chance, perhaps our only chance, to bring the Merchant to justice. We must not squander this opportunity as I doubt we shall be afforded another."

Chapter 18

As had become his custom of late, Holmes had eaten and left before I had arisen. I was sitting at the table, waiting for Mrs. Hudson to bring my breakfast, when the bell sounded. A second later, I heard the unmistakable tread of Wiggins ascending the stairs. As he began to pound on the door, I said, "Come in, Wiggins."

The boy entered looked about and realizing I was alone, said, "Blimey, Doctor. You're gettin' as good as Mr. 'Olmes at that deducin' thing. How'd you know it was me?"

Ignoring the lad's question, I replied, "Mr. Holmes is not here at the present. May I be of assistance?"

"Tell Mr. 'Olmes that one of my boys 'as the goods. I think 'e'll know what I mean."

"Is that everything?"

"You can also tell Mr. 'Olmes, I'll be outside The Prospect of Whitby, close by the river at 9. I should have more information for 'im by then."

"The Prospect of Whitby at 9. Righto, Wiggins."

The boy stood there looking at me, and suddenly I realized that he was hoping for some sort of remuneration. I reached in my pocket and pulled out some coins. "Here you are, my lad. And rest assured. I will relay your message to Mr. Holmes."

His "Thank you, Doctor" was followed by the usual cacophony as he descended the stairs, but he did refrain from slamming the door. "Halfway home," I thought.

I pondered the meaning of Wiggins' rather cryptic message, but decided, as Holmes might have postulated, I lacked sufficient data and did not have enough facts at my disposal to arrive at a conclusion.

With nothing else to busy me, I set about packing for the trip to Blenheim. I reasoned that I would need my formal evening attire in addition to a change of clothes for the journey home the following day. After making certain that everything I might require was in order, I decided that I might as well procure some reading material. After all, I reasoned, I had a three-hour train ride there, and once I arrived, I might be spending a great deal of time alone.

As I stepped outside, I felt the first few drops of rain, so I hailed a cab and directed the driver to take me to Hatchards in Piccadilly. At this venerable booksellers, I was able to obtain a splendidly bound English translation of Jules Verne's "From the Earth to the Moon." I had already read Wells' "The First Men in the Moon" and was curious to see how they differed. Well's work had been serialized in The Strand the previous year, and I had enjoyed it immensely although I found the notion of the gravity-defying cavorite, somewhat preposterous.

I also picked up a copy of Kipling's "Kim," which had also been serialised but in Cassell's, the chief competitor to The Strand. I had been a fan of Kipling's ever since I had first read his "Barrack Room Ballads," almost a decade ago. Pleased with my purchases, I returned to Baker Street, where I promptly pulled out my volume of Kipling's poetry.

I was so engrossed in my reading I never heard Holmes enter and was startled when all of sudden he declaimed:

"Though I've belted you and flayed you,

By the livin' Gawd that made you,

You're a better man than I am, Gunga Din!"

"Holmes, how on Earth could you know what I was thinking?"

He laughed and said, "As usual Watson, you give me far too much credit.

"I see the distinctive green bag that can only have come from Hatchards. In the bag, I spy a copy of 'Kim.' Those facts taken in concert with the fact that you are practically sitting at attention – something you do only when you are reading Kipling' 'Ballads' or Tennyson's 'Charge' – and the logical conclusion is Kipling, since your Tennyson volume is still on the shelf."

"I had picked up some reading for the train ride to Oxford, and with some time to kill, I started re-reading "Barrack Room Ballads.""

"Well, I think we might be better served by Mister Kipling's 'If' at this juncture."

"Yes, I can see that," I said, and then I added,

"If you can make one heap of all your winnings

187

And risk it on one turn of pitch-and-toss."

"That certainly sums it up rather neatly," said Holmes.

"Oh, by the way, Wiggins came by looking for you. He seemed disappointed that you weren't here, but he did say to tell you that one of his lads "'as the goods' as he put it," I said imitating Wiggins to the best of my ability.

The change in Holmes was dramatic. "Is he planning to return?"

"No. He said to inform you he would be outside The Prospect of Whitby tonight at 9."

"The Prospect of Whitby! Excellent! I know it well," replied Holmes. "We finally appear to be making real progress." Glancing at his watch, Holmes added, "I think Wiggins has surpassed himself in this instance."

"Shall I accompany you?" I asked.

"I fear not," said Holmes. "I think a proper gent like yourself might attract a bit too much attention."

"So then you are going in disguise?"

"I must," said Holmes. "If either of us were to be seen talking to Wiggins at that pub, both he and his cohort might be placed in jeopardy. They are risking enough as it is."

I understood Holmes' reticence, and I wondered if he realized he might be placing himself in danger.

We passed the rest of the afternoon going over the plans Holmes had made for the gala, refining some points and changing and adjusting others.

After dinner, Holmes disappeared into his room and about 30 minutes later, a rakish-looking dock worker emerged. He wore heavy black work boots, cheap grey trousers and a navy pea jacket that had seen better days. On his head, he had perched a blue watch cap and on his blackened hands, he wore fingerless gloves. He had greyed his hair and darkened his complexion, save for a nasty-looking pink scar that ran across his left cheek from ear to mouth. He had also blackened his teeth, and he seemed even taller than usual.

I was so taken aback by the sudden appearance of this wretched matelot that I exclaimed, "My word, Holmes! Your own mother wouldn't recognize you."

"I should hope not," he laughed. As he walked to the door, he turned to me and said, "I have no idea how late I will be."

"Do be careful," I said.

And then he was gone.

I remained awake until midnight, but Holmes did not return. As I lie in bed, I could feel the worry gnawing at the back of my mind. I knew that we were edging ever closer to, what I believed would be a final confrontation with the Merchant. I had faith in Holmes, but he had not come up against an adversary of this caliber since his fatal encounter with Moriarty.

When I awoke in the morning, I discovered yet another note from Holmes on the table.

Watson,

Things are coming to a head rapidly. I am not certain I shall see you before you leave for Blenheim. I do not know if you were planning to, but please pack your service revolver. I shall be in constant communication – one way or another.

S.H.

I saw nothing of Holmes until late Tuesday night. I was just preparing for bed when I discerned his tread on the stairs.

"Still up, old friend? Not waiting for me, I hope."

"Holmes, you are insufferable. Coming and going at all hours of the day and night."

"I can assure you it was most necessary," he replied.

"And keeping me in the dark?"

"As I have explained, that is for your own safety. Believe me, you will be under scrutiny at Blenheim, The smallest slip on your part could prove disastrous. It is as much for your own safety I do this as it is for the good of everyone else involved."

I nodded understandingly. "You know you have my full support, Holmes."

"Thank you, Watson." And then in a rare moment of candor, Holmes said, "I shouldn't be able to do this without your help, you know."

"Come now, you make too much of a small thing, freely given."

And then those few seconds of unabashed honesty, so rare in our long relationship, were behind us, and Holmes said, "Care for a nightcap? I know I could use one."

We chatted about various things as though there were no threats and the sense of rushing toward an uncertain future was held at bay – at least for that brief period of time.

As we rose to go to bed, Holmes said, "You may not see me, Watson, but you may rest assured I will be present."

In the morning, I breakfasted alone as had become my custom of late and around 9, I headed downstairs and after informing Mrs. Hudson, both Holmes I would be away for a few days, I hailed a cab and directed the driver to take me to Paddington.

As expected, the train ride took a little more than three hours, and I was once again glad I had purchased some reading material. I started with the Verne book, but I must admit that the idea of sending men to the moon by shooting them from a gigantic cannon left me shaking my head in bewilderment. I found it even more outlandish than the cavorite that Wells had employed.

So I put that book aside and enjoyed the views of the countryside, and when we pulled into the station, I descended to find Raymond waiting for me with his carriage once again. As he approached me, he gave me a broad wink and said, "It's so good to see you again, Dr. Johnson."

I was uncertain how to reply, so I waited until we were alone in the carriage. Before I could speak, he turned to me and said, "Those of us that met you when you were here last have received instructions to address you as Dr. Johnson."

"Holmes certainly thinks of everything," I reflected.

When we arrived at Blenheim, I saw a few other people taking in the grounds. I was escorted into the palace, where Childers was waiting for me, "Your room has been prepared. Lunch will be served in the dining room until three o'clock."

A footman led me to a room on the second floor that might have rivaled any of the best hotels in London. There was a sitting area with a small dining table and two chairs as well as several divans and armchairs. The bedroom area featured a large four-poster with crisp linens that had been bleached to a snowy white and pillows filled with eiderdown.

Childers indicated a bell pull, and said, "If you should require anything, simply pull, and one of the staff will be along to assist you presently."

I walked to the windows and discovered that I had a stunning view of the Italian Garden, which I later learned was the Duke's private garden. In the center sat a fountain, with a paved path surrounding it and two other paths bisecting the garden proper. Each of the four quadrants contained hedges that had been trimmed into an intricate design. Those hedges were bordered by paths on the outside and then encompassing all were two larger gardens, again with intricately designed and meticulously trimmed hedges.

"This is a far cry from Baker Street," I thought. Time permitting, I planned to explore the grounds and see what other secrets this estate harbored.

I had almost decided to skip lunch and visit the famed Rosamund's Well, which I knew was tucked away next to a quiet section of the Great Lake. Legend has it the Well was originally to have been a bathing place for the 'Fair' Rosamund Clifford, the mistress of King Henry II. According to historians, it had been constructed in the middle of the 12th century.

I suddenly found myself reflecting on how often this case had turned upon antiques from one country or another. I also recalled from somewhere that the area around the Well had been re-designed in the 1760s, and the Grand Cascade at the western end of the Great Lake is supposed to be one of England's most picturesque waterfalls.

However, as I passed the dining room, my nose was assaulted by a bevy of savory aromas. Before long, I was enjoying a bowl of mulligatawny soup and a mouth-watering salmon and leek quiche.

So delicious was the food that I lingered longer than I should have, and with high tea in an hour at 4, I knew I would just have time for a quick jaunt to the Well. When I arrived there, I must admit to being more than a little disappointed. The area was now overgrown and neglected. Still, the potential beauty was obvious, and I hoped the Duke would include this promising location in his restoration plans.

As I neared the palace on my return trek, I was approached by a young man of some 25 or 30 years of age. Shorter than I by several inches, he nevertheless carried himself with an air of absolute confidence. Thrusting out his hand, he looked at me and said, "Dr. Johnson, I presume?" Then he smiled.

"You have the better of me, sir," I replied.

"My apologies, sir. I am Winston Churchill, the Duke is my cousin."

"Ah yes, I have heard of you," I replied. "London to Ladysmith?"

"Yes," he answered, "I never expected those dispatches to be as popular as they are."

"They were quite good," I replied, "and now you are in Parliament?"

"I am," he said. "You seem quite well-informed as to my doings."

"That is part of my job," I said. Then I couldn't resist using that line from Holmes, "…to know things that others do not."

"At any rate," he continued, "The Duchess has informed me of your presence and she has hinted at her plight. I am quite fond of her, and should you require any assistance, you may count on me."

"Has she?" I asked.

"Yes, you see, my mother is American as is Consuelo, so we have that in common. You might say that we serve as each other's confidante."

I thanked the man, and promised we would talk at length. When I was alone, I thought, "This cannot be good. If the Duchess has told her husband's cousin, I wonder who else she might have informed. Holmes will not be pleased." However, since I had no idea where – or for that matter *who* Holmes might be – I had no way of informing him.

I put in a brief appearance at high tea, as I was no longer on solid footing as to who knew what. I ate quickly, but I learned that there would be another buffet at 8, with music, and the egg would be unveiled in the library at 9, followed by dessert and coffee in the Main Salon. Having refreshed myself with tea and a sandwich, I returned to my room, believing it best to keep as low a profile as possible.

After I had asked one of the servants to knock on my door at 7:15, I took what I thought would be a brief nap. I was awakened by the sound of a gentle tapping on my door and a voice repeating, "Dr. Johnson, it is a quarter past seven."

I thanked the lad and after splashing some cool water on my face, I began to prepare for the festivities. I had just tied my tie when it dawned upon me that tonight, this long battle of wits between Holmes and the Merchant would finally come to a conclusion.

As I reflected on the events that had brought us to this point, I realized how well the Merchant had acquitted himself against Holmes, and for a second I was plagued by doubt.

Then I thought of all the ne'er-do-wells Holmes had dealt with in his long career, including the bank robber, John Clay; the big-game hunter, Colonel Sebastian Moran; and, of course, "the Napoleon of Crime," Professor James Moriarty. Brilliant as they were, Holmes had bested all of them, and yet I must confess that niggling doubt refused to be silenced.

Chapter 19

If you are ever afforded the opportunity to visit Blenheim Palace, you will undoubtedly overwhelmed by its beauty as well as pleasantly surprised. Despite its age, the house has been equipped with all the modern conveniences, including central heating, electrical lighting and a telephone system, all of which were installed by the 8th Duke of Marlborough.

I mention these things because I learned that night the Long Library was to be lit with hundreds of candles instead of employing the electrical fixtures. The subdued lighting would certainly create a more intimate atmosphere, but I thought the shadows might afford a variety of hiding places should the Merchant decide to pay us a visit. I would have liked to communicate my misgivings to Holmes, but he had yet to make his presence known to me.

As I entered the dining room, I saw perhaps 80 people spread out in small groups. There was a festive atmosphere and a definite air of anticipation. The music was provided by a strolling violinist, and I wondered for a second if it might be Holmes in disguise. However, I quickly realized not even Holmes could shorten his stature by that much.

I was sipping a glass of champagne when an elderly man approached me. He walked with a cane, and as he reached for a glass from a tray held by a server, I saw that his hand shook quite badly. Turning to me, he said, "I am Robert Jordan. I was told that you are a physician, a Dr. Johnson."

"You have been well-informed," I said, "but few people here know me, so might I ask who told you about my profession?" I thought I was talking to Holmes, so I decided to keep the conversation innocuous. Yet, even though he stood less than two feet away, I was unable to tell for certain.

"I believe it was young Winston," replied Jordan, waving vaguely at the crowd. "Just out of curiosity your first name wouldn't happen to be Samuel, would it? I have always been a great admirer of the lexicographer."

Now, I was certain it was Holmes, and I was just about to let him know that I had caught on when a rather distinguished looking fellow approached us, "There you are Jordan; I have been looking all over for you."

"This is quite the evening, Your Grace," replied the man, and I suddenly realized that he was addressing the Duke of Marlborough. "Have you met Dr. Johnson?"

The Duke turned to me, extended his hand and said, "You must be a friend of Consuelo's. I am Charles Spencer-Churchill."

"I am pleased to meet you, Your Grace," I replied.

Turning back to Jordan, the Duke said, "I promised you an early peek at the egg. Are you still interested?"

"Of course," Jordan said. Turning back to me, the Duke said, "Would you care to join us, Dr. Johnson. It really is something to behold."

As we walked down the hall toward the Long Library, Jordan turned to me and said, "I am a collector. I have offered to buy the egg from Sunny," he said, employing the Duke's nickname as he gestured toward him, "but he refuses to sell."

Now I found myself wondering if I might be walking and talking with the Merchant. Thinking back to the incident in the British Museum, he seemed about the same height as the missing guard, though he appeared considerably older. Still, I had seen Holmes work the same magic, so I was determined to keep my guard up.

When we entered the Long Library, the Duke closed the heavy doors behind us. The room was illuminated by hundreds of tapers, arranged artistically in various candelabras that had been strategically placed from one end to the other. Directly opposite the entrance stood a square table, perhaps three feet wide and three feet deep. It had been positioned in front of the screen that closed off the alcove Holmes had mentioned.

The table had a rich, black velvet cloth on top, and directly in the middle of it stood the Duchess of Marlborough's Pink Serpent Egg. A single spotlight had been positioned above the egg, and it glistened under the bright illumination. As we approached, I heard Jordan inhale, and then he said, "It is magnificent."

The egg sat atop a triangular base of white enamel, and as the Duke pointed out one of the panels, the one facing us, had been emblazoned with his wife's monogram "CM" and a ducal coronet in diamonds. "As you can see," he continued, "the egg is also a clock."

Looking closer, I saw a diamond snake, curling up from the base. "The snake's head marked the hours, which had been set in Roman numerals also constructed of diamonds around the girth. In order to keep time, the egg turned within its framework.

"It is spectacular," enthused Jordan. "I simply must have it. I will pay whatever you ask."

"Sadly," said the Duke, "it is not mine to sell. However, you may try pleading your case with Consuelo although I would not be optimistic."

"I am told that she is quite attached to it," replied Jordan.

"It was made expressly for her," said the Duke. "Perhaps you can travel to Russia and have Fabergé construct one for you."

"Our climate is enough to endure. No, the thought of a Russian winter is enough to deter me from that – at least for the present."

All of a sudden, there was a light knocking at the door. The Duke went to it and opened it slightly to admit the Duchess and another man.

"We have just been admiring your egg," he explained. "I had promised Mr. Jordan a private viewing. You know, of course, he desperately wants to purchase it from you."

Resplendent in a white gown with silver beading, the Duchess smiled at Jordan, saying, "I am so sorry, Mr. Jordan. It is not for sale, but I can certainly appreciate your passion for something that blends art and function and, dare I say, genius."

Then nodding at me, she said, "Dr. Johnson, I am so glad you could make it. I trust your room is satisfactory?"

"Quite," I replied. Then speaking to both the Duke and Duchess, I said, "This is an extraordinary house."

"Yes," replied His Grace, "and in a very short time, I hope to have it restored to its full glory. And, now, my dear, who is this you've brought with you?"

"I would like to introduce John Eaton; he is going to play the organ for us tonight, and from everything that Lady Deborah has told me, we are most fortunate to have him."

I looked at Eaton, He was quite stocky, perhaps 50 years old and just about my height with a totally bald pate that glistened as if he had waxed it. His eyebrows were quite light, and his eyes were a light blue.

"You flatter me, Your Grace," said Eaton. "Now, if I may see the instrument. I have heard a great deal about it, and I should like to familiarize myself with it."

With that, he and the Duchess walked toward the great Willis organ at the far end of the room. As they departed, I heard him say, "I am so glad that you have a bare oak floor as it makes the sounds far more lively than floors covered with carpets."

201

Within a moment or two, I heard the first notes of Bach's "Toccata and Fugue," and I immediately realized that Eaton was no mere organist. The man was a virtuoso. He then segued into Poulen's "Concerto for Organ" and after several minutes, he began playing Pachelbel's "Canon."

I heard the Duchess enthuse, "That last piece is just lovely. That's the one I'd like you to play when the egg is unveiled." I was unable to hear Eaton's response, but I can only assume that he assented.

At that point, there was another gentle rapping on the door. The Duke said, "Come in," and Childers entered.

"Your Grace, it is almost eight. Shall I inform your guests that the library is now open?"

"Give us exactly one minute, Childers." The Duke then went to speak to the Duchess and Eaton at the organ, leaving Jordan and me to admire the egg by ourselves.

"It is stunning, is it not?" he offered.

I couldn't help but be impressed with the intricacy of the craftsmanship, and I told Jordan so.

At that moment, I heard a bell tinkle in the distance, and Childers announce, "Ladies and gentlemen, the library is now open." Before the first person had entered, the Duchess returned to the table and draped a black velvet cloth over the glass dome. "I want everyone else to see it at once," she explained.

The next hour was little more than tedious chitchat with people whom I had just met and who had made no lasting impression on me. Although I did spend a few pleasant moments in conversation with Winston Churchill discussing his association, and apparent growing discontent, with the Hughligans.

Finally, at exactly nine o'clock, the organist paused, the staff who had been passing champagne and various hor d'oeuvres discreetly moved to the rear, and the Duchess assumed her place near the table. As he and the Duchess had discussed, Eaton began to play Pachelbel's "Canon" in a very subdued manner.

When things had quieted, the Duchess said, "I would like to thank you all for coming. Although I am an American, I have the greatest respect for St. George, and that is why I have waited until now to unveil Carl Fabergé's latest creation, the Pink Serpent Egg."

With that, she removed the black cloth with a flourish, and the people closest to the table began to edge even closer as they "ooohed" and "ahhhed." As you might expect, there was a sudden crush near the table, but I was busy looking for the slightest indication of trouble. Needless to say, I saw nothing to indicate any type of disturbance.

After perhaps 30 minutes had passed and everyone had seen the egg, the Duke said, "May I have your attention?" When the room had quieted, he continued, "You may remain here marveling at the egg, or you may enjoy a rather sumptuous dessert table in the Main Salon. The choice is yours. The egg will remain on display until at least 11 should you wish to do both."

As you might expect, the room slowly began to empty of people. Although Holmes had wanted Lestrade to keep watch over one set of windows, I had not seen the inspector all evening; in fact, I had yet to catch sight of Holmes. When there were but a very few people left in the room, I walked to the other end of the room and quietly pulled a chair behind the base of the statue of Queen Anne.

Since no one had come to put the egg away, I was determined to keep watch over it and make certain nothing untoward happened. I pulled my chair closer to the base of the statue and angled it, so I could see the egg, and I thought no one could see me – unless they were really looking.

I sat there in absolute silence, doing my best to remain awake. Occasionally, a couple or two would venture back into the room to examine the egg, but the novelty of Fabergé's creation appeared to have worn off fairly quickly.

At about 11, the organist stopped playing and left, and I was totally alone in the room – or so I thought.

Chapter 20

Shortly before midnight, I was wondering how much longer I needed to continue my vigil. I must also admit that I was rather surprised that the egg had been left unattended.

Suddenly, I heard, rather than saw, someone enter the room. With my chair angled to face the egg, my view of the entrance was totally obscured by base of the statue. Nevertheless, I decided to peek around the base, and I caught sight of Eaton, the organist, walking toward the other end of the room. Once at the organ, he began to gather up his sheet music and place it in the satchel he was carrying.

I resumed my previous position and focused my attention on the egg once again. Then I heard another noise near the entrance and assumed the musician was departing. However, he seemed to be fumbling with the door handles, and there was an additional sound that I was unable to identify. About a minute later, Eaton came into view. He stood near the table with the egg, carrying a tray with two fluted glasses on it. He gazed at the egg, admiring it for perhaps a minute.

Then, he suddenly spoke, "Mr. Holmes, I know you are here somewhere. Won't you come out and join me for a glass of champagne? It really is a superior vintage." He paused and when no response was forthcoming, he spoke again, "Come now, Mr. Holmes, I recognized Dr. Watson earlier in the evening although I appear to have lost track of him. If he is with you, you can both come out. I will fetch a third glass."

I was stunned. When I had met him earlier in the evening, he had spoken with a proper British accent, perhaps from somewhere in the Midlands. However, now he sounded distinctly American.

He waited a few more seconds and then said, "Last chance, Mr. Holmes."

When there was no answer, he reached down and attempted to remove the glass dome but, for some reason, he seemed to struggle with it, and when he stepped back, I could see the dome was still guarding the precious egg.

Reaching into his satchel, he fumbled around and suddenly, he removed a pistol. Before I could say a word, he swung the pistol and smashed the glass with the butt.

What happened next occurred so quickly and was so baffling that it still amazes me. Although he had struck the dome with considerable force, it did not shatter. Even more amazing was the fact that although the glass had cracked, it had remained intact; however, the egg had disappeared from sight. And if that weren't enough, suddenly Holmes and Lestrade appeared from behind the screen that had been positioned in front of the alcove.

"So you are here," Eaton said. "I rather suspected you would be on hand. I mean leaving the egg unguarded, that's just not your style, now is it Mr. Holmes?"

Stepping forward, "Lestrade said, "I'm placing you under arrest," as he seized the gun and secured the man's wrist with a pair of darbies.

"On what charge? Damaging a glass dome?"

"Attempted theft at the British Museum..."

Before Lestrade could continue, the Merchant interrupted him. "Interesting, I don't remember ever visiting the British Museum, and I certainly don't recall trying to steal anything from it. I do hope that you have witnesses who can corroborate your allegation and state with certainty I was there."

Lestrade continued unruffled. "You are also charged with the murder of a man in Paris."

"A man, you say? Does the fellow have a name?"

"We will discover the victim's identity, soon enough," replied Lestrade.

"And someone saw me kill this unnamed man? I think you are treading on very thin legal ice, Inspector. However, I am more than happy to concede that this has all been some sort of misunderstanding. Now, if you would be so kind as to remove the cuffs immediately, I give you my word as a gentleman I shall not pursue legal action against you nor Scotland Yard."

Lestrade hesitated and then looked at Holmes, who broke his silence by saying, "It may take some time Mr. Bullard, but I promise you that you will pay for every crime enumerated by Inspector Lestrade, plus a few others he has yet to mention."

For the first time, I thought I detected an instant of doubt flash across the man's face, but his bravado remained intact as he said, "What did you call me, Mr. Holmes?"

"I called you Bullard. You are, after all, Charley Bullard, are you not?"

"Who the deuce is Charley Bullard?" asked Lestrade.

Gazing in my direction, Holmes said, "You can come out now, Watson. And I must say you did a splendid job, old fellow."

As I stepped out from behind the statue, Eaton looked at me and said, "So good to see you again, Dr. Johnson, or should I say, Dr. Watson. I was wondering where you were hiding."

"Holmes, just who is this impudent fellow? I asked.

"Gentlemen, allow me to introduce Mr. Charles W. Bullard. He is, as you can tell from his accent, an American. In addition to being one of the finest safecrackers in the world, Mr. Bullard is also a convicted thief and an escaped criminal. And I have no doubt, as Lestrade has said, that he is also a murderer.

"He was partners with a man named Adam Worth. Working in concert with one Fredericka Mandelbaum, Worth helped Bullard to escape from prison where he was serving a sentence for stealing $100,000 worth of goods from the Hudson River Railway Express.

"I have no doubt Mr. Bullard helped plan his own extrication as the scheme was quite ingenious. Worth, Mandelbaum and their associates rented an office directly across the street from the prison. Once they had the premises secured, they then tunneled into Bullard's cell. Of course, they had a little help on the inside from a pair of prison guards who were paid handsomely for their silence. That was, I believe in 1869.

"Never one to let grass grow under his feet, later that year Bullard and Worth robbed the vault of the Boylston National

Bank in Boston, getting away with some $200,000. However, the American police were determined to bring the robbers to justice, so Worth and Bullard decided to move to England. They have been living here under false names and quietly plying their criminal trade ever since.

"I cannot be certain, but I shouldn't be surprised if the body pulled from the Seine turned out to be Worth. Perhaps there was a falling out or a disagreement about the spoils."

"Bravo, Mr. Holmes. You appear to have everything figured out," said the man Holmes had called Bullard. "If I may, a question?"

"By all means," said Holmes.

"It took you long enough. What was it that finally tripped me up?"

"I have been aware of your activities for some time, but until you stole the *jambiya* from Lord Thornton, our paths had never crossed."

"I knew that job was a mistake from the beginning," Bullard said. "Adam insisted that it was an easy score."

"I might have even overlooked the theft," said Holmes, "but threatening a child is reprehensible."

"You still haven't told me what gave me away."

"I fully expected you to make an attempt on the Duchess' egg," said Holmes. "And when I heard of the failed attempt in Russia, I knew there was only one other place that you could obtain one.

"When the Duchess introduced you as John Eaton, my suspicions were pretty much confirmed."

"Oh?" said Bullard.

"You were entirely too predictable," replied Holmes.

I must have looked as mystified as Lestrade. "Holmes, Eaton is a common name I said."

"Do you remember how all the other names he and Worth used were those of men who had served in the Cabinets of different presidents of the United States? Well, John Henry Eaton was an American politician who served as a major during the War of 1812 and became an aide to General Andrew Jackson. In fact, Eaton fought with Jackson at the Battle of New Orleans.

"After the war, Eaton served in the U.S. Senate and was actually the youngest man ever elected to that august body. When Jackson was elected president, Eaton resigned his seat in order to serve as Secretary of War."

"That was my mistake?" asked Bullard incredulously.

"One of two," replied Holmes.

"What was the other?"

"Playing the organ. After all, there aren't too many criminals with the nickname 'Piano Charlie.' When I heard the first strains of Bach, I was absolutely certain that we had finally come face to face with the Merchant."

"The Merchant?" asked Bullard.

Smiling, Holmes said, "That has become Dr. Watson's sobriquet for you, Mr. Bullard. And now Inspector, you may take him away."

As Holmes turned away, Bullard said, "You disappoint me, Mr. Holmes."

Holmes stopped and looked at Bullard. "Oh, how so?"

"Did you really think I would undertake a job of this magnitude with but one bullet in my gun?"

"What on Earth are you talking about?"

"Mr. Holmes, as I am sure you know, these operations require a great degree of advance planning. There are always unforeseen elements that cannot be accounted for such as the presence of Inspector Lestrade and yourself behind that screen, not to mention the big officer lurking in the bushes outside. To quote the poet:

'The best laid schemes o' Mice an' Men

Gang aft agley,

An' lea'e us nought but grief an' pain,

For promis'd joy!'

If you catch my drift?"

I was surprised, for the man had delivered the lines written by Burns with an impeccable Scottish burr.

"I am certain I have no idea of what your 'drift' is," replied Holmes icily.

"Then let me spell it out for you. I know how fond you are of your landlady. What's her name? Mrs. Hill? Mrs. Haversham? Something with an 'H.' I am certain of it."

"Her name is Hudson," replied Holmes tersely.

"Of course, of course, Hudson. How could I forget a name like that? It was one of my biggest jobs. At any rate, how is the dear lady? Have you checked on her lately? I am inclined to think you have not, since you've been rather busy taking care of things down here."

I could not restrain my anger any longer, "If you have harmed Mrs. Hudson, not even the law will be able to protect you from me!"

"Easy there, Doctor. No harm has come to the woman – yet."

"What do you mean yet?" I roared.

"Quite simply this. If I do not make a phone call to a certain associate in London within," he glanced at his watch, "the next 10 minutes, you may well find yourselves returning to an empty house at Baker Street."

"So you are offering Mrs. Hudson's safety in exchange for your freedom?" said Holmes.

"Exactly," replied Bullard.

"Take him away, Lestrade, and make certain he does not escape. We wouldn't want anything to happen to Mr. Bullard before he can stand trial."

Even Lestrade seemed taken aback by the fact that Holmes seemed so resolute in his answer; as a result, he asked my friend, "Are you certain, Mr. Holmes?"

"I am," replied my friend.

I had felt ill when I heard Bullard utter those words, and I became more disconcerted as I watched Lestrade undo the chain that Bullard had used to secure the doors and march the man out of the library. I knew from the confident tone in Bullard's voice that this was no mere bluff. I also knew there was no way that we could return to London in time to secure Mrs. Hudson's safety. And even though Blenheim was equipped with telephones, I still was not certain a phone call, even from Lestrade or Holmes, would prove sufficient to foil Bullard's plot.

To say I was upset with my friend would be a gross understatement. I have often remarked how cold and calculating – and yes, even ruthless at times – he can be. I was so beside myself that I looked at Holmes and said, "I understand your need to uphold the law, but I never thought you would place an innocent life in jeopardy just to satisfy your own sense of justice."

Holmes actually seemed strung by my words. Softly, he replied, "As you should know by now, Watson, Bullard is not the only one who can plan ahead."

Chapter 21

Although my mind was racing and my heart was sick with fear for Mrs. Hudson, when Holmes uttered those words, I knew immediately that he would make things right. Inside, I was beside myself for doubting him, but given the ingenuity Bullard had demonstrated since our initial encounter, I believe I may be entitled to a measure of forgiveness.

"Do you remember when I went out to meet with Wiggins the other night?"

I could only nod.

"Although you have described me as an automaton, I am not devoid of feelings. I long suspected that Bullard might try to strike at me, and so far as I could tell, there were but three chinks in my armor – Mycroft, Mrs. Hudson and you.

"I immediately made Mycroft aware of the situation, and since then he has taken appropriate precautions with regard to his safety. I knew that you would be here with me, and while you are certainly capable of taking care of yourself, I also knew I would be on hand just in case things did go '*agley.*'

"If you remember, Wiggins' message for me was to the effect that his man had obtained the goods. That told me that one of the Irregulars had successfully insinuated himself in the Merchant's gang of, what shall I call them, the Marylebone Mercenaries? Fortunately, he had only been able to round up three or four dependable lads while Wiggins has at least 20 at his disposal.

"The plan was to kidnap Mrs. Hudson tonight, and hold her should anything go wrong here at Blenheim. So, Wiggins and I, with the help of Lestrade, smuggled several lads into the empty room at Baker Street, starting yesterday morning. They were joined in the afternoon by a brace of officers who posed as painters.

When the Mercenaries arrived at Baker Street earlier this evening, they were greeted rather rudely by the two officers as well as Wiggins and his cohorts. One of the would-be kidnappers is quite young, but the others will be treated as adults and punished for their crimes."

"How do you know all this?" I asked.

"I arranged to receive reports every 30 minutes from Baker Street?"

"But how?"

"You may recall that Officer Lawless was stationed outside in the bushes. Once the organ started playing and my suspicions were confirmed that Bullard was the Merchant, I opened the window slightly, and he has acted as a messenger both delivering my instructions to Baker Street via telephone and delivering the reports from Wiggins and the officers to me.

"That is why I could call Bullard's bluff without any hesitation. I knew that Mrs. Hudson was safe, and that Bullard's gang had been captured."

Inside I was so relieved, but then I said, "Still, you have some explaining to do."

"Do I?' asked Holmes.

Ignoring him, I asked, "First, how did you know where I was?"

"If you examine the folding screen very carefully, you will see three very cleverly disguised slits near the top that serve as peep-holes. I suppose they were originally intended to allow servants to discreetly anticipate when they might be needed. Together, they afforded Lestrade and me an almost unobstructed view of the entire room. When the crowd began to thin, I watched as you took up your position behind the statue."

"Oh. And why did you move Lestrade from guarding that bank of windows to taking up a position with you?"

"I could see there was only one hiding place in the room proper, and I was rather depending upon you to make use of it. That screen is perhaps 25 feet wide. I wanted to be able to surprise Bullard and surround him at the same time. So Lestrade joined me inside the alcove, and when the time was right, Lawless moved into the hallway right outside the entrance to this room.

"As you can see, it all fell into place rather neatly."

"Your plans often do," I said. "But what was all this hocus-pocus with the disappearing egg and the unbreakable glass dome."

"What an apt, term, Watson. For you see hocus-pocus is exactly what it was, and I must admit the idea germinated from a remark that you had made."

"Me?"

"Don't sound so surprised old fellow. I have often commented that while you yourself are not luminous, you are a conductor of light. Do you recall the night we took in that performance of *The Emerald Isle*?"

I nodded.

"The haunted caves in that play set me to thinking about magic. Then afterward, we drove right past the Egyptian Hall in Piccadilly, and you commented on the remarkable conjuring of Maskelyne and Cooke. And there it was."

"There what was," I asked, still totally befuddled.

"I needed to create an illusion. One that your Merchant would find irresistible. Look at the table on which the egg was sitting. It is what is known as a magician's table, and it was specially constructed for me by Mr. Maskelyne himself. Such tables often have what is called a 'well' – a secret compartment in which a magician may store those things he wishes to make appear and to hide those he desires to make disappear.

"The egg is inside the table – out of sight. Normally, you just place things in a well, but the egg was far too delicate, so I had Maskelyne construct a mechanical device, similar to those used to open pay toilets, that would open a door and gently lower the egg into the hidden compartment that had been lined with several layers of velvet and eiderdown to insure its safety.

"I also had a special dome constructed of Siemens glass that would not shatter at the first blow; however, it might not have withstood a second. So when Bullard hit the globe with his gun, the pressure from striking the glass activated the trigger Maskelyne had fashioned, causing the device to engage and carry the egg to safety."

"What if something had gone wrong?"

"You remember that you suggested the Main Hall as the room in which to show off the egg?"

Again, I could only nod.

"I opted for the Long Library for two reasons. First, because there is but a single entrance. But second and more important, because it has a wooden floor, unlike the marble one in the Main Hall. Bullard even remarked upon it when he entered with the Duchess, but he failed to recognize the significance of his own words. Were you to lift the edge of the cloth, you would see that the table has been bolted securely to the floor. The table itself, as well as the hidden cabinet, is made of sturdy metal, so in effect, the moment he tried to steal the egg, all Bullard did was succeed in moving it into a miniature vault."

"Holmes, you amaze me."

"I told you, Watson. I always have different plans in play – or bullets in my gun if you will."

At that we both chuckled.

A moment later, the Duchess entered. "I saw Inspector Lestrade leaving with Mr. Eaton in handcuffs."

Holmes then explained to her all about Eaton. When he had finished, she looked at him and said, "Thank God for that. And the egg, Mr. Holmes? Is it safe?"

Moving to the table, Holmes extracted a small tool from his vest pocket. Using it, he then removed the shattered globe. After that he then produced a key, inserted it directly into a hole in the table, and a few seconds later, the Pink Serpent Egg arose from the bowels of the table.

"Mr. Holmes, I do not know how to thank you."

"No, Your Grace. The English people owe you a debt of gratitude. Without your courage, cooperation and assistance, we might never have been able to capture Mr. Bullard and bring his reign of terror to an end."

The Duchess waved him off and said, "It was nothing. Any right-minded citizen would have done the same thing."

I was tempted to disagree with her but refrained.

"And now, Mr. Holmes. Is there anything I can do for you?"

"One thing only," said Holmes.

"Name it," she said.

"Do you mind if I smoke? I have been standing behind that screen with neither food nor drink for hours. I can go without nourishment for days, but not being able to smoke was most irksome indeed."

At that we all laughed, and Holmes immediately produced a cigarette and matches.

"You two gentlemen will stay the night," the Duchess instructed us, "and I am not taking 'No' for an answer. In the morning, we shall all enjoy a proper Blenheim breakfast. It is the very least that I can do."

I think both Holmes and I realized that arguing with her would be fruitless, so we chivalrously accepted.

Epilogue

Considering his rather colorful career both in London and abroad, the trial of Charles Bullard was carried out as a distinctly low-key affair. I suspected Holmes, Lestrade and certain other highly placed individuals went to great pains to make certain there was little if any press coverage.

After a very brief trial, Bullard was found guilty of all charges, including the murder of Adam Worth, and sentenced to Newgate. He was to be hanged later that year. His execution was scheduled for May 27, exactly three weeks after George Woolfe was hanged in the shed at Newgate.

Woolfe, you may recall, had battered and stabbed his girlfriend, Charlotte Cheeseman. On the night of 25 January, the couple was seen in a pub after which they went out onto the Tottenham Marshes where Woolfe stabbed her several times with a chisel. He was arrested two weeks later when he was found serving in the army under an alias.

There had already been rumblings about demolishing Newgate, and they swelled into a roar after his execution.

In an effort to recover Lord Thornton's *jambiya* and the Pyxis of al-Mughira, the government decided to offer Bullard a sentence of life in prison if he divulged the names of his buyers in those two instances. While Holmes was aghast at the possibility that Bullard might slip the noose and remained firmly opposed to the offer, he was given no say in the final decision.

Surprisingly, Bullard agreed rather quickly, and both the *jambiya* and pyxis were subsequently recovered and returned to their rightful owners. Propriety forbids me from naming the individuals who had purchased these items from Bullard.

As we neared the date for Bullard's transfer to Pentonville Prison, Holmes remarked one afternoon, "I am beginning to wonder, if justice will be served on Bullard in his new surroundings or if the rising tide of public opinion will prove a savior for all those destined to meet their maker at the hands of our penal system, whether it be by the noose or old age, and enable him to regain his freedom at some point in the future."

"Surely, that couldn't happen in his case," I said. "The public would be outraged."

"The public knows precious little about Bullard's activities," he reminded me.

Nevertheless, Holmes and I both kept a watchful eye as we waited to see what would befall Newgate and when the prisoners who remained incarcerated there would actually be moved.

One day about a week later, I heard the bell ring. I looked at Holmes and said, "I am not expecting anyone."

"Nor I," said he. "Perhaps this is a new client."

A few minutes later, there was a familiar rapping on the door. "Come in, Mrs. Hudson," Holmes said.

Our landlady opened the door and entered the sitting room. She was carrying a small package in one hand. "This just arrived for you by messenger, Mr. Holmes."

Taking the package from her, he said, "Thank you, Mrs. Hudson." He then placed it on the table and began to examine it from all angles. "I do not recognize the hand," he said indicating the block letters that spelled out "Mr. Sherlock Holmes, 221B Baker Street."

He continued, "Our sender has obviously taken considerable pains to disguise his handwriting. To what end, I wonder." Taking a small knife from his pocket, Holmes cut the cord that had been wrapped around the paper. "Ordinary twine. It might have been purchased anywhere." He then held the package between his thumb and index finger and carefully cut away the paper by running his knife along the slit.

"It has been glued," he said. "Again, the most common of adhesives and this paper yields nothing."

After he had removed the wrapping, he was holding a small wooden box perhaps six inches long by three inches wide and three deep.

Placing it back on the table with care, Holmes looked at me and said, "Now comes the tricky part. These boxes can be booby-trapped with all manner of deadly devices."

Taking the tongs and the poker from the fireplace, Holmes stood well back and cautioned me to do the same. Grasping one end of the box with the tongs, he used the poker to slide back the lid. When nothing happened, Holmes slid the lid completely off. As he turned the box on its side, I saw three small items roll out and come to rest on the table.

"What have we here," he said. After he had grasped one of the items with the tongs, I could see that he was holding a black king from a chess set. Setting it right, he then straightened up the other two pieces, still using the tongs, which I could now see were a white king and a white bishop. The pieces appeared to be made of ivory, and the carving on each was quite elaborate.

"They are beautiful," I said, "but what do they mean?" I asked.

"I am afraid they mean that evil is once again afoot," he replied.

"How so?"

"You play chess, Watson. What do these pieces tell you?"

"I am not certain I follow you."

"When you arrive at the endgame, there are certain combinations which can result only in a draw. Though white outnumbers black, two pieces to one, the rules of chess dictate the match must end in a draw. A white king and a white bishop cannot checkmate a black king.

"Consider, we – you and I – have recently brought to justice, a man who might well have been Moriarty's heir."

"You don't mean Bullard, the Merchant?"

"I'm afraid that I do," said Holmes. "I would venture to say that he has posited himself as the black king while you and I are the white bishop and king respectively."

At that, Holmes began to examine the box. "Holla!" he exclaimed. "What's this?"

He then withdrew a single sheet of white paper from the box. He remarked, "This was wedged in there so tightly it didn't fall out when I emptied the chess pieces, and I missed it on my initial observation." He then unfolded the sheet and read aloud:

It was an enjoyable match, Mr. Holmes.

Perhaps someday, we shall engage in another.

C.B.

"You do not think that Bullard has somehow managed to escape, do you?"

"No, Watson. I do not think he has escaped; I am certain of it. With everything that has been going on at Newgate, the pending transfers and the resources at his disposal, I am positive that Bullard, who was offered his life in exchange for providing the names of his customers, has escaped and is now a free man. Eventually, we will learn exactly how he accomplished that feat."

At that point, the bell rang. A few seconds later, I heard the sound of a heavy tread on the stairs.

Looking at me, Holmes said, "Unless, I am very much mistaken, I should be willing to wager that is Lestrade ascending the stairs as we speak, having decided to visit and deliver the bad news in person."

Author's note

The majority of the people and items mentioned in this book are based on real personages and artifacts. The Pyxis of al-Mughira remains on display at the Louvre, and you can still see the Tara Brooch at the National Museum of Ireland in Dublin. However, there was no *jambiya* belonging to a Lord William Thornton.

The history of the Fabergé eggs has been well-documented, and Consuelo Vanderbilt, the Duchess of Marlborough, was the first non-Russian to own such a treasure. As I have indicated, the relationship between the Duke and Duchess was not a happy one, and they separated in 1906 and were divorced in 1921. At the Duke's request and with Conseulo's assent, the marriage was annulled in 1926.

John Nevil Maskelyne was a prominent English stage magician, who really did invent the pay toilet along with other Victorian-era devices. Working with magicians George Alfred Cooke and David Devant, many of his illusions are still performed today. He also wrote "Sharps and Flats: A Complete Revelation of the Secrets of Cheating at Games of Chance and Skill," which was an instant hit and is still regarded as a classic gambling book. Together with his different partners, he performed at the Egyptian Hall for 31 years.

Also, there really was a safecracker and ne'er-do-well named Charles Bullard, who did flee America with his fellow criminal, Adam Worth, and took up residence in England.

According to what little is known about him, he was also quite a talented musician, who was nicknamed "Piano Charlie."

As for locations, Hatchards in Piccadilly is a well-known bookstore with a pedigreed history while Wilton's in London has always been renowned for its seafood.

Perhaps deserving the most praise is Blenheim Palace. Built in the early 18th century, it still ranks as one of, if not the grandest estate in England. The building and grounds have such a rich history that to do them justice might well require a book considerably longer than this one.

Finally, George Woolfe was the last man hanged at Newgate, which was closed in 1902 and demolished in 1905.

Acknowledgements

I continue to maintain that writing, at least as I practice it, is a lonely task. However, it has been made somewhat less onerous by the encouragement and patience of friends and family, who have supported and cheered me on in my endeavors.

I should be terribly remiss if I failed to thank my publisher, Steve Emecz, who makes the process painless, and Brian Belanger, whose skill as a cover designer is unmatched.

No book is complete without a solid line edit, and Deborah Annakin Peters provided that as well as a number of invaluable suggestions that improved the book immeasurably.

A special tip of the hat to Mark Stevens of Stevens Magic in Topeka, Kansas, who offered several options for making a small object disappear.

Also providing invaluable assistance was Dr. Alexa Frost, the archivist at Blenheim Palace, who answered all my queries about the history of that grand estate.

I also owe a considerable debt to Bob Katz, a good friend, who remains the finest Sherlockian I know. He has continued to encourage me and is kind enough to read my efforts with an eye toward accuracy – both with regard to the Canon, and perhaps more importantly, to common sense.

To Francine and Richard Kitts and Carol and Ron Fish, fine Sherlockians all, for their unflagging support and encouragement.

To my brother, Edward, and my sister, Arlene, who quite often had more faith in me than I had in myself.

Finally, to all those, and there are far too many to name, whose support for my earlier efforts have made me see just what a wonderful life I have and what great people I am surrounded by. So to all those who have read my earlier works, a sincere thank you.

To say that I am in the debt of all those mentioned here doesn't even begin to scratch the surface of my gratitude.

About the author

Richard T. Ryan is a native New Yorker, having been born and raised on Staten Island. He majored in English at St. Peter's College in Jersey City and pursued his graduate studies, concentrating on medieval literature, at the University of Notre Dame in Indiana.

After teaching high school and college for several years, he joined the staff of the Staten Island Advance. He worked there for nearly 30 years, rising through the ranks to become news editor. When he retired in 2016, he held the position of publications manager for that paper although he still prefers the title, news editor.

In addition to his first novel, "The Vatican Cameos: A Sherlock Holmes Adventure," he has written "The Stone of Destiny: A Sherlock Holmes Adventure" and "The Druid of Death." He has also penned three trivia books, including "The Official Sherlock Holmes Trivia Book."

In a different medium, he can also boast of having "Deadly Relations," a mystery-thriller produced off-Broadway on two separate occasions.

And if that weren't enough, he is also the very proud father of two children, Dr. Kaitlin Ryan-Smith and Michael Ryan, and the incredibly proud grandfather of Riley Grace.

He has been married for more than 40 years to his wife, Grace, and continues to marvel at her incredible patience in putting up with him and his computer illiteracy. They live together with Homer, a black Lab mix, who is the real king of the Ryan castle.

He is currently at work on his fifth novel, another Holmes adventure. He is hoping to follow that with a period piece set in the Middle Ages. After his hiatus from Holmes, he plans to take another look into the box he purchased at auction and see what tales remain.

Read on for an excerpt from the newest Sherlock
Holmes Adventure
by Richard T. Ryan

Through a Glass Starkly

There is a great deal of truth to the old adage: Time flies when you're having fun. When I first came into possession of Dr. Watson's tin dispatch box at an estate auction in Scotland several years ago, I reveled in my good fortune as I devoured the secret trove of untold tales that had fallen into my lap.

As I have indicated in the past, many were with withheld for personal reasons. Holmes' vanity can be seen as the primary cause for no less than five tales in the box failing to see the light of day.

At the other end of the spectrum, political considerations also played a prominent role in preventing both *The Vatican Cameos* and *The Stone of Destiny* from being published before now.

However, never were such considerations stressed as they were in the tale that Dr. Watson had titled *Through a Glass Starkly*. Given the events that shaped the narrative, it is no wonder that the good doctor wished to delay its publication for a very specific period of time, and now that time has arrived.

In what I can only assume is Doctor Watson's hand, a note attached to the first page of the tale makes it clear without the slightest bit of equivocation that the manuscript was to be shared with no one but the reader until a century had passed since the signing of the Treaty of Versailles, which occurred on June 28, 1919.

I have adhered to Dr. Watson's wishes out a sense of duty to a man for whom the phrase "Queen and Country" were far more than just words.

Although the events in this tale are now shrouded in the mists of the past, the instructions regarding the disposition of this manuscript were so explicit that to ignore them would be to do both him and Holmes a grave disservice.

That said, I hope you find the tale as fascinating as I do.

Richard T. Ryan

Chapter 1 – January 1907

I had neither seen nor heard from Holmes for several days. Normally, such a prolonged absence would not overly concern me, but Holmes had not even bothered to send a wire. He had informed me when he departed our lodgings a week earlier that he expected to be gone for an extended period, but there is a significant difference between "gone" and incommunicado.

And so it was with some relief on that Friday evening in late June I heard his familiar tread on the stairs. I noticed he was ascending quite slowly, and when he finally entered our lodgings, my joy at seeing my old friend was nearly offset by my concern for his appearance.

Always lean, Holmes now looked almost frail, His clothes hung loosely on his body and his face, always gaunt, now seemed more lined and sallow then I could ever recall.

I jumped up and said, "Holmes, what on Earth…"

However, he cut me off and managing a façade of bonhomie, clapped me on the back and said, "Watson, I cannot tell you how good it is to be home."

"Can I get you anything?"

"I should very much like a brandy," he replied.

"Have you eaten?"

"Not in two days."

"My word!" With that I rang for Mrs. Hudson. When she entered the sitting room, she took one look at my friend and said, "I'll be back shortly with some nourishment for Mr. Holmes."

Sipping the brandy that I had given him, I saw Holmes relax somewhat. Although I was curious, I refrained from peppering my friend with all the questions that were dashing about in my head. I knew that he would relate his adventures when he was ready, and there was nothing that could make him speak until he that time.

So we passed the minutes in a convivial silence, and then some 20 minutes later Mrs. Hudson knocked on the door and entered with a tray of sliced beef and a hearty brown gravy as well as half a loaf of freshly baked bread. "I was planning to go to the market tomorrow," she said, "so things are a bit short in the kitchen. If you'd prefer, I can prepare you some eggs and a rasher of bacon."

"No need, Mrs. Hudson," said Holmes with his mouth half full. "This is wonderful, but I do hope those eggs make their way up here in the morning."

"Indeed, they will, sir. And may I say, it's good to have you home."

With that, she curtseyed and left. Had she stayed another few seconds, she might have seen the beginnings of a blush creep into Holmes' cheeks. I watched as he ate. I have often remarked about my friend's seeming indifference to sustenance. All I can say after watching Holmes devour the beef and sop up the last bit of gravy with the bread is that every man has his breaking point.

Well-fed and reinforced by a second glass of brandy, Holmes settled in his chair and reached for his old clay pipe. I watched as he filled it with shag from the Persian slipper, and a few minutes later it was as though he had never been gone.

After several more minutes had passed, he looked at me and said, "I suppose some sort of explanation is in order."

I merely smiled, and said, "That is entirely up to you."

He nodded and then said, "You know the state of affairs in Europe at the moment."

"All too well, I'm afraid."

"At the moment, there is another Peace Conference being held in The Hague. The heads of state are hoping to reach some accord regarding the conduct of war. As I am sure you know, this second conference in The Hague was originally scheduled for 1904, but had to be postponed because of the war between Russia and Japan."

"How ironic that a peace conference should be delayed because war had broken out."

Holmes cast a wry look in my direction. "Indeed," was all he said.

"As a result of the Russo-Japanese war, the Japanese have emerged as a force with which to be reckoned on the world stage."

"True," I said, "Russia had the opportunity to save face and bring the war to an early resolution, but convinced of its superiority, it pressed on and suffered a number of humiliating defeats. But what has all of this to do with you?"

"I have from time to time spoken of the power my brother wields within the government."

"Unless I am mistaken, you once said of Mycroft that 'Occasionally he *is* the British government,' adding that at those moments, he is 'the most indispensable man in the country.'"

"Bravo, Watson! Well, this is one of those moments. Mycroft hand-picked the delegates to the conference, and he has been in constant contact with one or another of them since they departed for the Netherlands."

"My word!"

"Yes, however, apparently shortly after their departure, word reached my brother that an attempt would be made on the life of one of the French representatives, and all the evidence would point to the German delegation."

"But to what end?"

"To push Europe closer to the precipice of war and possibly over the edge."

"But if the Germans were not the ones behind the attempt, then who was it?"

"That is where things get murky," said Holmes. "Mycroft had been provided with a code name for the assassin, Atlas, but little else. He immediately made me aware of the problem and tasked me with foiling the assassination attempt. He wanted me to travel to The Hague and serve as a sort of bodyguard for the French.

"I explained that it would be impossible as it was highly unlikely the French delegates would constantly be in each other's company – both day and night.

"Mycroft understood that and said he wanted me on the scene, so that when he learned the identity of the would-be assassin he would have a man in place. He also told me that everything I was doing was top-secret."

"So that explains why I didn't hear from you."

"I am afraid my hands were tied," said Holmes, who then continued, "I arrived in The Hague six days ago and found a cable waiting for me at my hotel."

"Had Mycroft learned the real name of the assassin?"

"He had but rather than risk putting it in a telegram, he sent me a clue."

"What on Earth do you mean?"

"The telegram contained but two words 'Flambé pied-à-terre.'"

"A flaming apartment? What on Earth was Mycroft thinking?"

"Actually, Mycroft was being quite clever, and banking on the fact that I would be up to the task."

"So you were able to discern some secret meaning in his rather cryptic message?"

"Indeed. The fact that he wrote the text in French had me thinking of that country immediately. Apparently, Mycroft had learned the assassination would take place in Paris rather than The Hague. I immediately boarded a train for Paris and some 15 hours later I arrived at the Gare du Nord."

"And the flambé pied-a-terre?"

"You still haven't figured that out? Although many Parisians are aware of its existence, I am not certain how far that little secret has spread in the rest of the world."

"Dash it all, Holmes. Can you not come to the point? What secret?"

"Mycroft was alluding to the Eiffel Tower in his own cryptic way."

"The Eiffel Tower? But why?"

"It seems that when the tower was built, Monsieur Eiffel constructed a small apartment for himself near the top."

"My word! Well, that explains the inclusion of the phrase pied-à-terre, but surely it was not on fire?"

"No," Holmes laughed. "You correctly translated the word *flambé* as flames, or as we would say 'burning.' However, Mycroft needed an extra layer of deception in case the cable happened to be read by the wrong eyes, so he dropped the last 'e' from *flambeé*, which translates to 'soaring.' I must confess it took me some few minutes to figure out my brother's intent, but once I divined his meaning, I understood he wanted me to find a 'soaring apartment.' Fortunately, I knew of one, and I believe it to be the only one that fits Mycroft's description."

"So you headed to the Eiffel Tower?"

"Yes. When I arrived, there was a man standing near the base of the tower. I recognized him immediately even though he was doing his best to appear inconspicuous. Apparently, he also was acquainted with me because he approached me and said, 'Monsieur Holmes, I have been waiting for you. I was beginning to wonder if perhaps something had happened to you.'

"I smiled and apologized for any inconvenience I might have caused him."

"'Think nothing of it,'" he said. 'I have been requested to give you these,'" he said, handing me an envelope. 'Now, if you will excuse me, I think my work here is done. I am leaving tomorrow for Greece, and I shall be gone for at least a month.'

"What was in the envelope, Holmes?"

"A letter that I could produce in case my presence at the tower was questioned, and a set of keys."

"You don't mean…"

"I'm afraid I do. Gustave Eiffel had just turned over the most exclusive residence in the City of Lights to me."

"But why?"

"I rather suspect in some capacity Eiffel is in league with Mycroft. Be that as it may, I was more interested in what I might find in the '*flambeé pied-à-terre.*'

"And what did you discover?" I asked.

"After ascending nearly to the top of the tower, I made my way to the apartment which I entered to discover a fully stocked kitchen and another missive from my brother.

"And what did Mycroft's letter say?"

"The assassin, Atlas, had been positively identified as an Austrian nationalist named Stefan Lorenz. Mycroft said he had other agents trying to learn anything they could about Lorenz.

"According to Mycroft, Lorenz is a former military man who was dispatched to China as part of the multi-national force that sought to quell the Boxer rebellion. He seems to have been quite the soldier, reveling in the plunder and bloodletting that followed the siege of the Legations. Once he was separated from the Austrian army, he became a soldier-of-fortune and eventually began to hire himself out as a killer.

"Although there was no photo of Lorenz, something that did not totally surprise me, there was a rather detailed description that was actually quite pointless, for in the description he is described as a master of disguise."

"Sounds rather familiar," I grumbled.

Holmes looked at me and then grinned, "Yes, in a very real sense, I suppose you could say I was hunting myself. I had just finished perusing Mycroft's letter for a second time, which also instructed me to make the apartment my base of operations while I was in Paris, when I thought I heard a very soft knock at the door."

"When I opened the door, there was no one there. The only person in sight was a woman who was just entering the lift to descend.

"Assuming the wind must have blown something against the portal, I closed it and then I noticed a letter on the floor."

"A letter, you say?"

"Yes, I can only assume it had been slipped under the door by the woman."

"What did it say?"

"Here you may read it yourself." With that Holmes pulled a sheet of paper from his jacket pocket and handed it to me.

After I unfolded it, I saw a single line of gentle cursive in an obviously feminine hand. I read it over three times, looking for clues, and then I turned to Holmes. "What does it mean?"

"I think it means exactly what it says, 'Lorenz uses a crutch.'"

Kickstarter

A big thanks to all our Kickstarter backers. Kickstarter is an important part of setting up and marketing new book projects and the following people supported the project with a mention in the book:

Steve

Gina R. Collia

Melissa Aho

Steve and Sue Dietrich

Wayne Miller

John Gigante

Hilton Flores

Paul Hartnett

Jack Griffin

Jim Jorritsma

Eric Schaefer

Christopher Davis

CPSIA information can be obtained
at www.ICGtesting.com
Printed in the USA
BVHW040328021020
590078BV00004B/266